SHERLOCK HOLMES:
A DUEL WITH THE DEVIL

Moriarty! He was, according to Sherlock Holmes, 'the Napoleon of crime' — a mathematical genius gone mad who was the thinker and organizer behind nearly every great crime that came Holmes' way. Why then was the evil professor so seldom mentioned in Dr. Watson's previous accounts of the Great Detective's exploits? Now Watson finally tells all in this newly discovered manuscript. And he even admits to a shameful role he unknowingly played in one of Moriarty's most nefarious schemes — as the would-be assassin of Sherlock Holmes!

ROGER JAYNES

SHERLOCK HOLMES: A DUEL WITH THE DEVIL

Complete and Unabridged

LINFORD
Leicester

First published in Great Britain in 2003 by
Breese Books Limited, London

First Linford Edition
published 2004
by arrangement with
Breese Books Limited, London

British Library CIP Data

Jaynes, Roger
　　Sherlock Holmes: A duel with a devil.—
　　Large print ed.—
　　Linford mystery library
　　1. Holmes, Sherlock (Fictitious character)—
　　Fiction 2. Watson, John H. (Fictitious character)
　　—Fiction 3. Detective and mystery stories
　　4. Large type books
　　I. Title
　　813.6 [F]

　　ISBN 1–84395–502–4

Published by
F. A. Thorpe (Publishing)
Anstey, Leicestershire

Set by Words & Graphics Ltd.
Anstey, Leicestershire
Printed and bound in Great Britain by
T. J. International Ltd., Padstow, Cornwall

This book is printed on acid-free paper

If I tell you, Watson, in all seriousness, that if I could beat that man, if I could free society of him, I should feel that my own career had reached its summit ... But I could not rest, Watson, I could not sit quiet in my chair, if I thought that such a man as Professor Moriarty were walking the streets of London unchallenged.

Sherlock Holmes,
The Final Problem

Preface

Moriarty! Has any name in the history of our realm ever been so untouched by scandal, and yet so synonymous with evil? Has anyone, save Jack the Ripper, played a more sinister role in London's sordid history of crime?

'The Napoleon of crime,' my good friend Sherlock Holmes once called him,' . . . the organiser of half that is evil and of nearly all that is undetected in this great city. He is a genius, a philosopher, an abstract thinker. He has a brain of the first order. He sits motionless, like a spider in the centre of its web, but that web has a thousand radiations, and he knows well every quiver of each of them. He does little himself. He only plans. But his agents are numerous and splendidly organised. Is there a crime to be done, a paper to be abstracted, we will say, a house to be rifled, a man to be removed — the word is passed to the professor, the matter is organised and carried out. The agent may be caught, in that case money is found for his bail or his defence. But the central power which uses the agent is never caught — never so much as suspected.

At the time Holmes first uttered such praise of the man,[1] privately I was a bit sceptical. I thought his opinions far too generous. And yet, looking back over the years, perhaps the best testament to Moriarty's insidious genius is that his name is mentioned so few times in all my public accounts of Holmes's various adventures.

The blame for that, of course, must finally be shouldered by me, my famous companion's Boswell. How many times, after the darbies had been applied and the criminals escorted into a waiting van, had Holmes suddenly remarked, 'You realise, of course, Moriarty was at the bottom of this,' and then proceeded to tell me why. And yet, repeatedly, it was I who chose to edit such closing remarks from the final

---

[1] *The Valley of Fear*, January, 1888.

text at the time of publication, primarily for fear of such legal repercussions as Holmes himself had noted at the time of the tragic Birlstone affair.[1]

Now, I feel, such worries are past. Moriarty lies long dead beneath the swirling waters of Reichenbach Falls. The heretofore untold details of his evil career need no longer be suppressed. I can now state, without hesitation, that Moriarty and Holmes crossed swords many, many times before their final climactic encounter at the Falls, though the professor's behind-the-scenes role was seldom mentioned. One case that immediately comes to mind was the previously published *The Red-Headed League*, in which, I can now reveal, the infamous forger John Clay and his accomplice were actually operating on Moriarty's behalf. So, too, was James Ryder, head attendant at the Hotel Cosmopolitan, who, after Holmes discovered his bungled attempt to steal the Blue Carbuncle, fled the country more in fear of Moriarty's wrath than any loss to his

---

[1] *The Valley of Fear*, January, 1888.

good name. Two other cases, I should add, occurred in that same year, which Holmes refused to allow me to publish at all — *The Pauper's Good Fortune* and *The Destruction of Culverton House*. In both instances, my companion felt that I could not recount the facts involved without pointing a tell-tale finger in the direction of one of his many informants. Moriarty's revenge, we both knew, would have been swift and sure.

I must, of course, truthfully admit that Holmes did not — in spite of his formidable powers — always come out the winner. What an ingenious fellow, Moriarty. He was, I am forced to confess, an overpowering, at times almost omnipotent force, which seemed to pervade London as thoroughly as the dense yellow fog on a damp November day.

For almost six years prior to Moriarty's death, it seemed that his lieutenants, his minions, his thugs, were everywhere. No sooner would Holmes thwart one of their clandestine attempts at murder, blackmail, arson or extortion, than another sorrowful client would appear at our Baker Street lodgings, pouring out his or her singular story of woe. Which, after some reflection and investigation on Holmes's part, we invariably found was the result of a scheme designed and carried out by either Moriarty, or his ruthless chief of staff, Colonel Sebastian Moran.

Yes, for almost six years — far longer and more frequently than I dared reveal at the time — Holmes and Moriarty duelled, thrust and parry, like two sword-bearing protagonists, for what at times seemed like the very heart and moral soul of London.

Now, glancing back in retrospect over my voluminous files, I find that the Holmes–Moriarty struggle was never fiercer than during the autumn and early winter of 1888, when in a period of approximately two months' time, Holmes found himself challenged by no less than three of Moriarty's most nefarious schemes. I was, I am proud to say, an eyewitness to his remarkable performance in them all — though I shall forever be ashamed of my initial (albeit unintentional) role in the last of the episodes chronicled here.

In all our years together, I doubt if we were ever confronted by a more sublimely menacing foe than Moriarty. It shall always be to Holmes's credit, as these adventures illustrate, that he was able through his supreme intelligence and unique methods of deduction to foil — often though not always — the diabolical designs of Moriarty, who was in the final analysis, a mathematical genius gone mad.

Dr John H. Watson
London, England
October 7th, 1920

The Case of the Dishonoured Professor

During the third week of September, 1888, I was persuaded to undertake a personal matter for a boyhood friend who resided near Stranraer, the small seaside village of my youth, located off the Firth of Clyde on the hilly, wind-swept west coast of Scotland.

Upon enquiring, I was pleasantly surprised when Mr Sherlock Holmes, who rarely strayed beyond London's drab environs, agreed to accompany me on what I thought was sure to be an arduous journey, citing the need for a few days of sunshine and fresh ocean air to revive his spirits.

Holmes, at that time, had good reason to feel both physically and mentally drained. In the previous two weeks, he had not only solved the peculiar case of Bishop Henley's bloodthirsty parrot, but also thwarted an attempted train robbery at Paddington Station, and engineered a daring rescue of the Home Secretary's son from the hands of a desperate group of kidnappers — an act which, I would be remiss if I did not add, saved Inspector Lestrade's reputation in the process. Holmes was, to coin an oft-used phrase, played out — the result of too many days and nights without proper nourishment or rest. Far too often, during that hectic fortnight, he had spent countless hours ruminating in his favourite armchair or pacing restlessly before the fire from midnight till dawn, smoking pipeful after pipeful of the strongest shag imaginable while his precise and penetrating mind mulled over the convoluted matters at hand. As was his habit, he would allow his mind to work on a problem without rest, turning it over, examining it from every possible point of view, until he had either fathomed it or decided that his data were incomplete. In the latter case, I found, he would have invariably gone out again on some particular errand by the time I had risen the next day.

'To let the brain work without sufficient data is like racing an engine,' Holmes had told me, many times before. 'It will, my dear Watson, unless given a rest, tear itself to pieces.'

Naturally, I was aware that Holmes possessed considerable reserves, both physical and mental. And yet, seeing how heavily he had drawn upon them during the last two weeks, I feared he was, at that particular moment, dangerously close to the breaking point. Little wonder, then, that I heartily welcomed his unexpected companionship on my trip to the north, and not only because I knew it would make my journey much more bearable. The sun and sea air, I also felt sure, would do Holmes a world of good. A week or so away from Baker Street would free him, at least for a time, from the increasingly excessive strain his singular profession demanded.

My part in my childhood friend's affair turned out to be simple enough: a half-hour's testimony before a local magistrate trying to decide who, among seven feuding heirs, should receive what portion of a considerable (especially by Scottish standards) inheritance. Getting to Stranraer, however, was a far more tedious task, requiring a full day's ride north by train from London to Carlisle, near the Scottish border (where we spent the night), and a second trip by rail west towards the coast the following morning. During that three-hour sojourn on the Glasgow and South Western Line, we passed first through Dumfries, the city of grim coalfields in which Robert Burns had died, and then made our way on across the rolling moors and rocky cliffs of the Southern Uplands, until we finally arrived — tired, but no worse for wear — at the bustling little harbour town of my birth.

Holmes, as was his habit when travelling by rail, was a virtual recluse the entire way, burying his nose into the latest editions of whatever newspapers were available, and taking long naps as well. I, quite fortunately, had remembered to bring along a favourite volume of sea stories, and concentrated my thoughts upon it.

For three days after I had given my testimony, Holmes and I remained in Stranraer, enjoying a sort of busman's holiday. Upon the advice of my friend, we had taken a small, but comfortable, upper room at the King's Arms (reasonably priced, I felt, at three shillings and sixpence a day), which offered us a magnificent view of the entire harbour area, as well as the approaching sails of the big ships, as they made their way up the oft-times choppy waters of Loch Ryan toward Stranraer, their next port of call. From our landlord, we learned that steamers daily afforded tourists what was then the shortest sea-passage possible to Ireland — across the North Channel to Larne in just two hours — but such an excursion was not what Holmes and I sought just then. Instead, each morning, we were content to rise late, enjoy a hearty Scot's breakfast of porridge and cakes, and then spend a relaxing afternoon walking the beaches north of Black Head Light. As we thus savoured the benefits of the unusually mild weather and bracing salt air, I regaled Holmes with tales of my ancestors, one of whom I have always believed was an officer aboard a Spanish galleon, which, my father once told me, had crashed against the jagged rocks in that vicinity on a stormy night some three hundred years before, at the time of the Armada's defeat.

Holmes's initial reaction to my claim of some shred of Iberian heritage was one of polite scepticism. Until, on the second day of our wanderings, as he was wading barefoot along a stretch of tawny, wind-whipped beach, his toe unearthed a tarnished, worn doubloon from the sand.

'Aha, Watson!' he cried out, with the first hearty laugh I had heard in weeks. 'Come here!'

As I drew closer, he tossed the coin to me. 'Even here, by chance, I seem to have solved a mystery,' Holmes remarked, with some amusement, as I stared down at the coin's eroded features in my hand. Clasping my shoulder, he added, 'Come along, old fellow. You now have more than sufficient proof, I believe, to convince any future unbelievers.' A mischievous smile crossed his lips. 'Consulting detectives notwithstanding.'

I beamed. Not out of vindication, but because I realised that my friend's good-natured remarks were the first clear sign his period of prolonged lassitude was near an end.

By the fourth day, Holmes was once again his usual energetic and restless self — a good sign, I felt — and his appetite and good spirits seemed restored. Over breakfast, he declared himself rested and fit, and we decided forthwith to leave for London on the morrow. As I helped myself to yet another of our lady's tasty kippers and a second helping of porridge, Holmes surprised me by proposing a different return route home: why not, he suggested, rise early and take the train cross-country not only as far as Carlisle, but on east to Newcastle and south to Durham as well? According to his ever-handy Bradshaw's, the connecting links of the North British line could have us there no later than one o'clock.

'But for what reason?' I enquired. 'If our destination is London, Durham is, most certainly, out of our way.'

'For that half-day's inconvenience,' Holmes explained, 'we shall have the entire afternoon free to view a medieval group of structures unrivalled in all of England. Come, come, Watson! Such trips as these are rare. What better way to conclude our splendid vacation than with a visit to that historic city, with its mighty cathedral on the Wear? Whose walls Scott called, 'Half Church of God, half castle 'gainst the Scot'.'

Naturally, I agreed at once. Holmes had always been an avid student of English history; his renewed interest, I felt sure, was yet another sign of his recovery. Besides, his point was well taken: Durham's great cathedral and castle, along with their adjoining monastic buildings, were a landmark of the realm I had yet to see.

Hence, on the following day, a Monday, we rose with the sun and left Stranraer at half past seven, switching trains at Carlisle for Newcastle, which we made in just over two hours, despite half-on-demand stops at Hexham and

Corbridge. Another change of trains — with an accompanying half-hour's delay — was required before we could begin the final leg of our journey south to Durham. That was how, on that particularly bright autumn day, we found ourselves forced to pass some time in the decidedly dingy and somewhat malodorous confines of Newcastle Central Station.

'A rather drab place, wouldn't you say, Watson?' Holmes said, as we settled ourselves on one of many hard, pew-like benches that had been placed about the grimy terminal.

'That appraisal, I think, is extremely kind,' I replied, amidst the smoke and the noise of the dreary, unkempt station. 'Why, the sanitary conditions here are nothing short of disgraceful — as I'm sure your trained eye has already noticed.'

'Oh, really?'

'Quite so. The rubbish bins are overflowing, and look at these old papers and wrappings littering the benches! And yet, Holmes, I see not one — not one! — janitor or charwoman about, with a pail and mop in hand.'

'Indeed.'

'Look here,' I continued, retrieving a discarded sheet from beneath our bench. 'Saturday's edition, Holmes! Why, it's clear to me this station has not been properly cleaned in days.'

My companion chuckled, as he drew out pipe and pouch and proceeded to fill the bowl. 'An accurate deduction, my dear Watson,' he concurred, a faint smile of amusement upon his lips. 'Why, I do believe that you are finally applying my methods correctly, after all.'

'I find nothing humorous in this,' I declared, irked at my friend's apparent indifference.

'There, there, Doctor — bear with it! Another hour, and we shall be enjoying not only a fine autumn afternoon, but some of the most interesting buildings in Europe, whose construction marks England's first great step from the Romanesque to the Gothic! True, a long train-ride awaits us tomorrow, but by nightfall, we shall most certainly be back at our lodgings in Baker Street. Which, I have no doubt, will have become miraculously clean and neat as a pin in our absence, thanks to the industrious Mrs Hudson.'

'Well, I do hope that industry includes a hearty dinner, to celebrate our return. Pheasant and oysters, perhaps? Long travel, I have found, does stimulate the appetite.'

Holmes chuckled once more. 'Never fear, Watson. I have, already, anticipated your Epicurean desires. You recall I took time to despatch a telegram, when we changed trains at Carlisle? It was to our good landlady, informing her we should arrive at St Pancras at six tomorrow night, and to expect us shortly thereafter.'

'Excellent! In return, I shall now purchase what dailies are available, before we board our train. I am not unmindful of your travelling habits, Holmes, and unless I'm mistaken, that is a vendor's booth, in front of the booking office down the way.'

'I'd rather you didn't, just this minute,' my friend replied. He struck a match, and carefully held it above the bowl of his black clay, inhaling deeply as he spoke. 'A visit by you to that kiosk might, I am afraid, frighten away our extremely attentive friend.'

Looking up, I caught sight in the crowd of a short, stocky man in a brown suit and dark bowler hat, newspaper in hand, who was pacing somewhat furtively back and forth between the booking office and a large baggage wagon, which was sitting next to the tracks about half the distance away. He appeared to be watching us closely.

'Yes, I see him, Holmes. The bulky fellow with the game leg.'

'Worse than that,' my companion said. 'An amputee.'

'However can you tell?'

'Observe his shoes, Watson. The right one is wrinkled, the left one smooth.'

'But what could he possibly want with us?'

'I've no idea, but we do seem to have attracted his interest. He first caught sight of us as he turned round from purchasing his newspaper, about the time we took our seats. He has since spent the last few minutes observing us intently.'

'Perhaps he's one of the Chapel crowd,' I suggested, recalling Holmes's recent success on behalf of the Home Secretary. Instinctively, I reached into the pocket of my coat. 'Revenge, perhaps? If so, I have my revolver ready.'

'Thank you, Watson, but I doubt that you shall need it. His features do not appear malevolent; rather, he seems beset by indecision. For whatever reason, he is at present trying to decide whether or not to approach us.'

An expectant look suddenly crossed Holmes's hawk-like face. 'Well, well!' he exclaimed. 'Our mysterious friend, it seems, has made up his mind. Look! He's coming our way.'

A moment later, the burly fellow stood before us, hat in hand, a look of apprehension upon his broad, open face. Deep brown eyes punctuated his ruddy countenance, which was framed by bushy brows, a full head of chestnut hair, and thick Dundreary sidewhiskers. While his broad shoulders and muscled arms spoke of great strength, he did not appear threatening; hence, I loosened my grip upon my revolver.

'You are Mr Sherlock Holmes?' he asked, with some hesitation.

'That is correct,' Holmes answered him, 'and this is my friend and associate, Dr Watson.'

Relief flooded the man's heavy features, as he reached out and nervously shook both our hands. 'What a remarkable turn of good fortune!' he cried, drawing a train ticket from the pocket of his waistcoat. 'As you can see by this, I have saved myself a considerable journey. My plan, sir, was to catch the London express, in order to seek your advice. And now, instead, I find you here in Central Station!'

'How interesting that you should recognise me,' Holmes remarked, 'since I am certain we have never been introduced.'

'Quite so. You were pointed out to me by a friend, at the Café Royal, when I travelled down on business almost a year ago. Dr Watson was with you at the time. It was not until I was able to glimpse his face as well that I felt confident enough to enquire.'

'So we observed. Now, if you would be

so kind — why do you wish to consult me?'

The man appeared taken aback. 'Why, because I am Jonathon Thatcher of Durham, sir! Younger brother of the ill-fated and unfortunate Professor Aubrey Thatcher, of that same city.'

It was obvious the man felt that the mere mention of those two names would explain his presence before us. Yet I could tell by Holmes's impassive stare that they meant no more to him than me.

'But you mean that you've not heard?' the big man asked. 'Why, man, it's the talk of Palace Green! A scandal at the university, they say! Lord knows, there's been little else in the papers these last two days!'

'We have been in Scotland, upon another matter, for a time,' Holmes rejoined. 'I know nothing of your brother, Mr Thatcher, and very little of you — save that you are a bachelor, a cobbler by trade, and only this morning sat in the barber's chair before you began your journey. I do feel, however, that this must be a serious matter, to so greatly disturb a former trooper of the 10th Hussars, who has given a leg in service to the Crown.'

Thatcher's jaw dropped. For an instant, I thought his paper and hat might do the same. 'Lord help me, if you aren't a magician!' he declared, shaking his head in wonder. 'Why, I've only just met you, Mr Holmes. How come you know so much of me?'

'It is no trick, I assure you,' Holmes explained. 'Most people see, Mr Thatcher, but do not observe. I do both, and draw my conclusions directly.

'For example, the third finger of your left hand is bare, yet there is no lightening of the skin to suggest it has ever worn a ring. Your trade is also clearly indicated by the condition of your hands — the bruised thumb and fore-finger of the left, and the dark stains upon the fingertips of the right? The first, most likely, were caused by errant swings of the hammer; the second from years of applying boot polish to leather that no soap or scrubbing could erase. What else, save a cobbler, could such a combination suggest?'

'And the barber?' the other asked.

'That is the easiest of all, told by the small, clipped hairs so evident upon your shirt collar — and, I might add, a rather excessive application of Rosewater.'

'I see,' the fellow concurred, ' — But here! How then did you fathom my military history?'

Holmes pointed his smouldering pipe in the direction of Thatcher's right hand. 'Only a 10th Hussars' man would sport such a tattoo,' he answered, referring to the dark blue words 'Don't Dance Tenth' which peeked from beneath Thatcher's shirtcuff. 'Were you Watson's age, I should suspect you saw service in Afghanistan. The recent campaign in the Sudan seems more likely. How you incurred your wound, I've no idea, but your stiff walk and smooth left shoe immediately suggested an artificial limb, as you paced back and forth among the crowd. The faint creak of metal as you bent forward to shake my hand confirmed it.'

'You are correct again, sir,' the stocky man admitted. 'It happened at El Teb, with Graham in '84, of which I'm sure you've read. We had been ordered to relieve Tokar, when quick as a cloud passes over the sun, six thousand of the wuzzies descended on us. The rifles of the British square were too much for them, of course. It was only when we pursued them through the brush that heavy casualties were incurred.

'Three of the black devils came at me, as I rode slowly past a thicket; I shot them all, but my frightened horse reared up and took a spear. As I clung onto the reins, a Dervish woman rushed forward, brandishing one of those hatchets they used to finish off our wounded. As she lunged, I did for her as well, but her axe caught me full across the thigh. Both horse and I went down — the next I knew, I was writhing upon a stretcher, being attended by a doctor.'

'How awful!' I interjected. 'Mr Thatcher, you have my utmost sympathies, indeed.'

'No need,' he insisted. 'I was one of the lucky ones that day. Two thousand wuzzies died in the dust and heat — as well as a hundred of our men. You have been in the field, Dr Watson. To do your duty and get through, as you well know, is what matters in the end — else we would not be conversing now. Besides, Lord knows, I'd give up my other leg, would it ensure the return of my dear brother.'

Holmes perked to attention. 'Ah, he's missing then?'

'Three days. Since Friday night, to be exact.'

'And you have heard nothing from him?'

'Not a word.'

'But has there been no sort of communication? No note, for example, to confirm an abduction?'

'None.'

'H'mm. Then I think we can discount a kidnapping. Most certainly, you would have received demands by now. Very well, Mr Thatcher. Since we obviously have some time, please do lay the facts before me. But pray, be precise! Like a doctor, I must know every symptom, before a diagnosis can be made.'

'The facts are these, Mr Holmes. My brother, Aubrey Thatcher, has been a professor of mathematics at the University of Durham for some years. His career, I might add, has been a quite distinguished one. Last spring, in June, his exemplary service was duly rewarded, when he was appointed to fill a seat on the Senate — an honour which, he admitted to me, was one he had long desired but felt, for whatever reasons, was beyond his reach. He was to have been confirmed this very week, as is the custom, with the opening of autumn classes — '

'A joyous occasion, I am sure,' Holmes commented.

'There's far more to it than that,' the big man persisted. 'You see, my brother had also confided to me that on the day of his confirmation he planned to publicly announce his betrothal to one Miss Ann Lowell, a young lady with whom he had struck up an acquaintance in the spring. Like myself, my brother has been a lifelong bachelor; so, in spite of some modest reservations, I could not but feel overjoyed when he told me such news. This week, I felt, should have been the happiest of his life, Mr Holmes. I only tell you this, because it makes — to me, at least — what occurred on the night of Friday last seem all that much more puzzling and bizarre.'

Holmes frowned deeply. It was a look I had seen before, when things were not progressing quite as rapidly as he would have liked. 'And just what did happen, Mr Thatcher?' he asked.

'A few minutes after seven on that night, my brother left his house on Ashgate Road, after informing his house-keeper, Mrs Clarridge, that he had an important appointment to keep, but that he probably would not be late. As she later told the police, she was quite surprised by his sudden announcement, since a wicked storm was brewing, and because my brother — who is normally very conscientious — had mentioned nothing of it earlier in the day.

'Friday being her night off, Mrs Clarridge had planned to attend the theatre as was her habit. Instead, because of the foul weather, she decided to stay in, and retired to her room to read. As you might well imagine, she was even more surprised when my brother returned at approximately nine-fifteen, went immediately to his room, and minutes later reappeared with a suitcase in hand and walked out the door, into the night.'

'He gave no explanation?' I asked.

Thatcher shook his head.

'And what of Miss Lowell?' Sherlock Holmes enquired. 'Was she able to shed any light upon the matter?'

'Yes, but hardly in the manner which I had hoped,' the other replied. 'You see, she disappeared that night as well.'

Holmes uttered a low whistle of surprise. 'I see,' he murmured, placing a finger to his lips. 'And did they — ?'

The muscles of Thatcher's adurate jaw stiffened. 'Apparently, yes.'

For a long moment, we all said nothing.

'The following morning,' Thatcher continued, 'I called at the Albert House, just off Crossgate Avenue, where I knew Miss Lowell was staying. Like you, I had hoped she might provide some clue as to my brother's strange departure. When I enquired of the landlady, Mrs Purcell, I was told that Miss Lowell had checked out the previous evening at around eight o'clock, and that she had left no forwarding address. Naturally, I was amazed.

' 'That cannot be,' I told her, identifying myself. 'Her engagement to my brother, Professor Aubrey Thatcher, was to have been announced within the week.'

' 'Then it's hardly as strange as you might think,' she shot back, with more sarcasm than I cared for. 'For it was with him she left last night. Rolled off in a fancy four-wheeler, they did — after he'd been sure to settle her bill!' As I'm sure you can understand, Mr Holmes, I was deeply shocked.'

'Then it does appear they left together,' Holmes stated, thoughtfully. 'And you have no idea why?'

An anguished look appeared upon the face of our unusual client; his broad shoulders rose and fell, as he put forth a heavy sigh. 'You must excuse me, Mr Holmes,' he said, finally. 'I am not a faint-hearted man, but this is the most damning explanation I have ever been forced to give. I would only ask, as I tell you the rest, that you do not judge my poor brother prematurely.'

Holmes gave the man a look of exasperation. 'At this moment, Mr Thatcher, I am neither judge nor jury,' he declared. 'I am merely a consulting detective — who wishes to hear the facts! Pray, proceed.'

'Very well. On the morning after my brother's disappearance, the body of Arnold Samuelson, a clerk at the Mathematics Library in Blakeney Hall, was found lying across the tracks at Lydney Station. As you might expect, the body was horribly disfigured, as a number of trains had passed through during the night. What remained of it had been carried quite some distance; an arm and a leg were discovered at separate locations, each having been severed completely.'

'How awful!' I interjected. 'But how then was the body identified?'

'According to the newspaper accounts, it was simple enough. The police retrieved a wallet belonging to Samuelson from between the tracks, and were also able to match the colour of the victim's hair and his approximate height and weight. In addition, the article stated, a Mr Thomas Feeny, who had spoken with Samuelson earlier the previous evening, recognised the suit of clothes he had been wearing and a large signet ring, taken from the right hand of the body.'

'And who is Thomas Feeny?' Holmes asked.

'The chief clerk at Blakeney Hall. Samuelson's supervisor.'

'A terrible accident, admittedly,' I observed. 'But what has it to do with your brother, and his disappearance?'

'Elementary, Watson,' Sherlock Holmes explained. 'Samuelson had spoken to Feeny just hours before his death. And, unless I'm greatly mistaken, that conversation concerned Professor Aubrey Thatcher — and, most likely, that important meeting he was determined to attend, despite the inclement weather.'

'You are quite right,' Jonathon Thatcher confirmed. 'At the time Feeny identified

Samuelson's body, he also turned over to the police certain documents Samuelson had left with him for safekeeping on that very night, when he stopped by Feeny's rooms shortly before seven o'clock.'

'Documents?'

'Yes. Papers which proved — although I still cannot believe it — that my brother was guilty of a grave indiscretion, at the time he received his doctorate, more than a decade ago. According to Feeny, Samuelson had discovered that my brother had — for lack of a better word — plagiarised much of his doctoral thesis from one written by another student some years before. And that, upon confronting my brother upon the matter, he had been threatened with his life, unless he remained silent. That, he told Feeny, he had done, although reluctantly, for almost two months' time.'

'Go on,' Holmes said.

'Samuelson, Feeny told the police, had decided he could keep quiet no longer. His conscience, he said, simply would not permit it. How, after all, could a man with such false credentials be allowed to sit upon the Senate? He was, he said, on his way to speak with my brother a final time that very night, to offer him what he felt was the only compromise possible, given the circumstances. In light of my brother's threat, he felt the documents in question should remain with someone he trusted, just in case.'

'A compromise, you say?' Holmes questioned. 'And what were its conditions?'

'That my brother decline the honour of the Senate, giving whatever excuse he deemed necessary. In return, Samuelson promised to say nothing of his past wrong-doing, thus allowing him to retain his chair at the university.'

'And if your brother refused?'

'Then, according to Feeny, Samuelson was prepared to lay the facts before Professor Cromwell, Dean of the Mathematics College, and the local newspapers as well. You can well imagine, Mr Holmes, what the result would have been.'

'Your brother's disgrace would certainly have been considerable,' Sherlock

Holmes agreed. 'He would have forfeited not only his seat upon the Senate, but his professorship as well. Then, too, there would have been Miss Lowell's reaction to consider.'

'Exactly. Little wonder then, after hearing Feeny's story, that the police began to look at things quite differently. Originally, they had assumed Samuelson's death to be accidental, though there was some question as to why he had been walking so near the tracks. A second examination of his body, however, revealed a bullet wound just beneath the heart, and a .32 calibre bullet lodged next to the spine. Their subsequent visit to my brother's home found him to be mysteriously absent, and a search was immediately conducted — '

'At which time, the gun was found.

'Yes. In the corner of his bedroom closet. The calibre matched and one cartridge was spent. The police say it had been fired recently.'

'The weapon is your brother's?' I enquired.

'Without a doubt, Doctor. I have

another which matches it exactly. They were gifts from our late father, at the time we each came of age.'

Thatcher dug again into the pocket of his waistcoat, this time extracting a small, folded scrap of paper. 'It is a copy,' he said, as he handed it to Holmes. 'The original was discovered inside the pocket of Aubrey's smoking jacket, when the police searched his home. Naturally, they were not about to allow me to carry it down to London.'

Holmes unfolded the note and read:

Professor Thatcher,
I can remain silent no longer. Meet me in the park near Lydney Station at seven-thirty Friday with the money.
Samuelson

Holmes whistled again. 'This does appear to explain it all,' he said. 'Were I the police, I should suspect that Samuelson was blackmailing your brother, and your brother shot him, and then dumped his body upon the tracks in hope of concealing the murder. After which, he fled with Miss Lowell.'

'That is the belief of Montgomery Doyle, the chief of the Durham police,' Thatcher replied. 'It is also, I regret to say, a theory which the newspapers have given considerable credence.'

'Your brother's accounts — they have been checked?'

The other's gaze fell. For a long moment, he refused to speak. 'They have,' he admitted, finally. 'And it was discovered that on the morning prior to his disappearance my brother withdrew a considerable sum of money. Five thousand pounds, to be exact — all but a modicum of his savings. As yet, it has not been accounted for.'

'I see.'

After uttering those two words, my companion lapsed into silence, staring intently down at the scrap of paper he had only moments before just read. He was, I knew, oblivious not only to Thatcher and myself, but to the noise of the busy terminal which surrounded us. Not a flicker of emotion crossed his long face, as he contemplated the matter at hand.

'This note, and the pistol, would seem to incriminate your brother greatly,' he mused, at length. 'The handwriting on the original, I take it — '

'Was positively identified as Samuelson's,' Thatcher said.

'Have you any idea when he received this note?'

'I know exactly. Mrs Clarridge told me it was delivered by messenger at three o'clock on Thursday afternoon. She left it, as well as the day's post, in the study upon his desk.'

'And did your brother leave the house on Thursday night?'

'According to Mrs Clarridge, he had a dinner engagement with Miss Lowell.'

'At which time,' Holmes suggested, 'he might conceivably have pleaded his case — and convinced her to leave with him the following night.'

'That, too, is the opinion of the police.'

'And what do you think, Mr Thatcher?' Sherlock Holmes asked. 'Is your brother capable of such acts? Is there such a dark side to his nature?'

The big man thought a moment before

answering. 'Some would say Aubrey and I were as different as two brothers could be,' he replied, matching Holmes's direct gaze. 'From childhood, our interests differed. I was good with my hands; he worked with his mind. I became a cobbler, he a professor. Given that, our social circles could hardly be expected to cross. Still we've always remained close, and I do know my brother well. He is a kind and intelligent man, if a bit naive in some ways. In my heart, I do not believe he could bring himself to steal from, much less kill, a fellow man.'

Holmes reached out and placed a hand on the big fellow's shoulder. 'Then I suggest, Mr Thatcher, that you exchange your ticket for a fare to Durham at once,' he told him, 'so that you may accompany us to your fair city. I had planned to spend my afternoon viewing the relics of St Cuthbert. Instead, I shall investigate your case. Even more than the cathedral, it piques my curiosity.'

Thatcher leaped to his feet, grabbed my friend's hand, and pumped it vigorously. 'I have not the adequate words to thank you, Mr Holmes,' he declared fervently. 'Never fear, I shall defray any expense — '

Holmes silenced him with a raise of his hand. 'We can speak of that later,' he said. 'If my watch is correct, you have not much time. You have luggage to transfer, surely.'

As Thatcher strode off, I felt compelled to offer a word of caution to my friend. His vacation from crime, I felt, had been far too brief. 'Holmes, must you climb back into harness so soon?' I asked. 'The purpose of your accompanying me, after all, was to gain respite from such problems as these.'

'Tosh, Watson! I'm fit as a fiddle.' Holmes brought out his pouch and proceeded to make a new pipe. 'But, come now, what do you make of all this?'

'After hearing the particulars, I am astonished you agreed to take the case,' I declared.

'Ah, you think his brother is guilty, then?'

'I do. Holmes, it's plain as day. Aubrey Thatcher was on the brink of ruin. His only solution was to kill Samuelson, disguise the crime, and flee with the Lowell woman to parts unknown. America would be my guess.'

'Then answer me one question, Watson. If Thatcher planned to kill Samuelson and flee, why did he withdraw five thousand pounds from his account?'

'My dear Holmes, it's obvious. He needed the money to finance a new start, once he'd fled the country.'

'In that case, why not withdraw it all? Would you flee with only a part of your savings and leave the rest behind?'

'Perhaps Thatcher didn't intend to kill Samuelson,' I countered, defensively. 'Perhaps he asked for more money, they quarrelled, and Thatcher shot him in self-defence.'

'A possibility. But if Thatcher intended to pay, it's unlikely he would have brought along his own gun. And if the killing were accidental, he would hardly have had time to notify Miss Lowell, so she could be waiting obediently, luggage in hand, in the lobby of her hotel.'

Holmes struck a match and began to

fill the air above us with clouds of blue smoke, as he silently considered the problem one more time. 'It just won't do, Watson!' he concluded. 'My every instinct tells me this case is just too pat. Too many facts — which on the surface appear conclusive — simply do not ring true. Of one thing, however, I am certain: Professor Thatcher withdrew that five thousand pounds in an attempt to buy Arnold Samuelson's silence.'

'And how, pray, do you know that?'

'Because of the note Thatcher received from Samuelson on Thursday afternoon. And, because of what he told Thomas Feeny on Friday night.'

'I don't follow you. The two seem to disagree.'

'My point, exactly. When a man sends a blackmail note one day, and says his life has been threatened the next — what are we to believe?'

'That which happened first, I'd say.'

'Correct, Watson. Samuelson did not meet Thatcher that night to work out any sort of benevolent compromise. He was there for the money. Feeny's testimony merely confirms him to be a liar. More importantly, it casts suspicion upon the so-called forged documents he possessed.'

'But why did he confide in Feeny at all? Why not merely hide the documents instead?'

'The answer, I think, is obvious. Samuelson was taking great pains to create some sort of alibi — but for what reason?'

'To conceal the fact that he was blackmailing Thatcher?'

'If so, he failed miserably. The note, remember, was written in his own hand. On top of which, he went out of his way to reveal a motive, by taking Feeny into his confidence. It's almost as if — ' Holmes frowned. 'Something has been cleverly done here, Watson,' he added. 'Much, I suspect, has been revealed only to conceal.'

'And what, do you think, happened to the five thousand pounds?'

'I confess I have no idea. We know only that the money was not on Samuelson's person when he met his gruesome end, else the police surely would have discovered it. — Ah, but our happenstance client returns! Accompanied, I see, by an able porter with his bags. You will excuse me, Watson? I think I shall just have time to purchase the latest dailies, before we get under way.'

'And dispatch another telegram to Mrs Hudson,' I reminded him, as visions of a pleasant and plentiful supper back at Baker Street faded from my brain.

Our half-hour train ride south across the sunny ridges of the Pennine Chain passed quickly, during which time I recounted to Jonathon Thatcher some of my own military experiences, first as a surgeon attached to the Fifth Northumberland Fusiliers, and later with the Berkshires at Maiwand. Holmes sat silently in his corner of the compartment the entire way, hidden behind sheets of newsprint, smoking his pipe contentedly. While Thatcher and I conversed, we also satisfied our hunger (Holmes naturally refused) with large sandwiches and tea, taken from luncheon baskets we had purchased at the station prior to boarding.

Upon arriving, Holmes dashed outside

the terminal and strode briskly off down the Lydney Station tracks, leaving us to account for our luggage and hail a cab. By the time we emerged, he was already returning our way, a discouraged look upon his lean face.

'Alas, it is as I feared,' he commented. 'Anything which might have been of use has been obliterated. More trains have passed through, and there are footprints everywhere — the police, no doubt.'

Holmes raised his hand before us. 'I did, however, find this torn scrap of cloth, next to the rails. Samuelson's suit, perhaps? Also the bushes next to that far turn in the road are broken down quite badly. I suspect it was where the body was dragged on to the tracks.'

After securing a conveyance, Holmes stood a moment at the kerb, directing his attention to the small park on the opposite side of the street. Then suddenly, we were off, following him across the sunlit green, dotted with the first brown leaves of autumn. Moments later, we found ourselves before a white roof-covered bandstand some hundred yards from the station.

'I have no doubt they met here,' Holmes said, gazing at it up and down.

'And how do you know that?' Thatcher demanded.

'Where else would one man wait to meet another on such a stormy night?' Holmes replied. 'Look around. There is no other shelter. And from this distance, a shot would not likely be heard, given the wind and pouring rain.'

Quick as a cat, my companion sprang up the bandstand steps, then carefully stepped inside. 'Aha!' he cried. 'Look here!'

The white board floor was covered with muddy footprints. Holmes motioned us to remain outside, upon the steps, then pulled out his glass and fell down to his knees.

'There are two sets here in the middle,' he said, as he carefully edged about. 'One set with a square toe, one set round. Square-toe has a loose nail in his left heel. He was here the longest, pacing back and forth. Waited a considerable time, I'll wager, given these cigarette stubs. Yes, they met about here, and their talk most certainly animated.'

'How can you tell?' I enquired.

'Because, from there to there, the footprints go this way and that, constantly overlapping.'

'And what of these?' I asked, pointing with my stick to the muddy marks at the entrance. 'And these, upon the steps?'

'Some are theirs, surely,' Holmes replied, almost without interest. 'Some may be from the police, if they were sharp enough to enquire. At any rate, they are all too smeared to tell. But this — '

Holmes crawled to the far side of the bandstand floor, where he now lay almost prone, his magnifying glass less than an inch above the floor.

'Look at it, Watson!' he cried, as he edged his way back towards us. 'The lines, Watson! The two black lines!'

The early afternoon sunlight had started to make its way across the bandstand floor. Squinting hard, I could make out two long scrape marks, slightly faded now, which drew two thin muddy lines from where Holmes had lain right to my very feet.

'The proof,' Holmes said, 'is conclusive. The shot was fired there. After which the body was dragged across the floor to this top step, where it was hefted and carried away.'

Glancing up, I could see our client had been much affected by my companion's conclusions. Holmes, it seemed to me, might just as well have struck him across the face.

'I take it then, sir, that you concur with the police,' he said stiffly, his cheeks flushed.

Holmes seemed genuinely surprised at his remark. 'Were that the case, Watson and I should bid you good day, and board the next train south to London,' he replied. 'Calm yourself, Mr Thatcher. It is always a capital mistake to act until you possess all the facts. These, I admit, are not in your brother's favour. But until I have many more at my disposal, I am not prepared to render an opinion.'

'My apologies, Mr Holmes,' the big man rejoined. 'You realise, I'm sure, that this is an emotional turmoil for me. You are here at my behest and upon my brother's behalf. In the future, I shall do my best to restrain my personal feelings.'

'Well, then, enough said. Do you know of a hotel where we might stay? Something close to the university grounds would probably suit us best.'

'I do. The Rose and Crown, in Market Place, just north of the castle and Palace Green. An old-fashioned place, but comfortable enough, I assure you. I doubt securing a room will be a problem on a Monday.'

'Then I suggest we go there at once and deposit our bags. Is your brother's house far from there, Mr Thatcher? It would be, I feel, an excellent place to continue our investigation.'

'Why, of course, Mr Holmes. It's only a short ride from your hotel, just off Palace Green.'

A half-hour later, our four-wheeler was clattering across Durham's historic Framwellgate Bridge, as we crossed the sparkling waters of the River Wear to reach the curled-finger peninsula of land that made up the heart of the city. Before us was spread a breathtaking panorama of ancient England — the majestic Durham Castle, beneath whose flags was housed much of University College, and off to the right, University Library and the huge cathedral itself, looming above the river, its western towers and the stone columns of the Lady Chapel below shining white in the bright, midday sun.

'What an imposing sight, Holmes.'

'Quite so, Watson. How can anyone not be impressed by such a regal structure? It is clearly one of the finest examples of early rib-vaulting to be found in Western Europe today.'

'I see you are quite knowledgeable of your Norman history, Mr Holmes,' Thatcher remarked. 'You have visited Durham before, then, I take it?'

'Unfortunately, my appreciation of the cathedral has, until this moment, come only from books,' Holmes admitted. 'This is, you must realise, a treat for me. I have always felt that no man can understand himself or his times, without sufficient knowledge of those which have preceded him.'

My friend turned a penetrating gaze in

Thatcher's direction. 'In that vein, there is an avenue I wish to pursue,' he suggested.

'But of course. Proceed.'

'You mentioned earlier that your brother was naive in certain matters. I suspect your reservations concerned his relationship with Miss Lowell.'

'Let us just say that I did not fully approve of my brother's involvement with the woman,' Thatcher answered. 'She was, I felt, decidedly below his station.'

'And why do you say that?'

'Call it intuition, Mr Holmes. Call it anything you choose. The course of my life, I must admit, has allowed me some experience where the opposite sex is concerned. Far more, certainly, than that of a sheltered university master. Miss Lowell, quite frankly, struck me as more of a courtesan than a lady.'

'Good gracious!' I exclaimed.

'In my brother's company, she was charming, polite, given at times to almost maudlin shows of affection. Yet, on more than one occasion, I noticed how carefully she observed his reactions, as well as those of his friends and associates.

There was calculation in that look, Mr Holmes. The kind you might receive were you to stroll down Haymarket after dark. The woman, I felt, sought something more.'

'Your brother's money, perhaps?' Holmes suggested.

Thatcher cleared his throat. 'Yes.'

'An understandable reaction, given the circumstances. Protective, of course. And you told your brother as much?'

'I certainly did not. Since he seemed happier than I had ever seen him, I could not bring myself to interfere. Had I voiced my concerns, I have no doubt it would have caused a rift between us.' Thatcher glanced away for an instant, squinting up at the bright midday sun. 'It was my belief — and still is — that his infatuation with a woman twenty years his junior had, unfortunately, over-ruled his sense of judgement.'

'I see. And can you describe her for me?'

'Miss Lowell is an attractive woman. I can well understand why my brother — or any other man, for that matter

— might be taken with her. She has fair skin, hair the colour of honey, and always is dressed stylishly. But the most striking thing about her is her eyes.'

'And why is that?' I asked.

'Because they are the deepest, clearest blue I have ever seen. It is the reason, I imagine, why she invariably wears some shade of that particular colour.'

For an instant, a cloud seemed to cross my companion's face. 'Blue, you say?' he asked. 'Always?'

'Quite so. She has a regular penchant for the colour. Electric, azure, Dresden, even navy. The shade may vary, but without exception her dress and hat — and oft-times her gloves, as well — are some tone of blue. But why do you ask, Mr Holmes? The point seems trivial to me.'

'Perhaps,' my friend concurred, 'but I have found it a mistake to disregard anything when investigating a crime. The smallest point may often be the most essential.'

As we had conversed, I noted our cab was slowly making its way north along Silver Street, a busy venue which brought us presently to the entrance of Market Place. The large square immediately brought to mind London's Covent Garden, since it contained row upon row of wagons and stalls, from which proprietors were hawking their wares. Turning left, we traversed the edge of the bustling, noisy place, past vendors whose shelves and counters offered poultry and pork, fresh vegetables and fruit, casks of wine, and even bright flowers arranged in pots and wicker baskets. Reaching the other side, our cab rolled to a halt before a brown limestone frontage, whose faded crimson-and-gold awning proclaimed it to be the Rose and Crown.

'One final point, Mr Thatcher,' Holmes enquired, as he stepped down to the kerb. 'What do you know of Miss Lowell's background? Has she an occupation?'

'Not that I'm aware. As to family, she did once speak of a late brother in Surrey, who left her some investments.'

'They must have been considerable,' Holmes mused. 'A woman with such a bent for wardrobe must, after all, have means.'

Aubrey Thatcher's home was one of three handsome red-brick houses situated neatly in a picturesque close in the heart of the university grounds, just south of the castle and within easy walking distance of the giant University Library. Large oaks framed the house and shaded the small front lawn. Beneath the front windows, hedges grew, and dark green ivy had been allowed to creep its way to the window ledges of the second storey. Noisy thrushes greeted us as we started up the walk, splashing in the large, sculpted bird-bath and then flitting quickly out of sight.

As we reached the front step, Holmes paused. 'Has it rained since the night your brother disappeared?' he asked.

'Why, no.'

Holmes knelt down, his glass in hand. Next to the side edge of the concrete step, the dried front half of a footprint was pressed into the clay. 'Observe,' he said, 'the toe is square. Mrs Clarridge has swept since this was made, else the back half, too, would remain. A misstep surely — '

'By someone in a hurry,' I conjectured.

'Or,' Holmes said, 'who did not know the way.'

Our ring was answered by a small, wiry woman I took to be the housekeeper, whose silver-grey hair was drawn severely back into a bun. At first, she eyed Holmes and me apprehensively, a large broom clutched in one hand. Upon seeing Thatcher, however, she heaved an audible sigh of relief and swung the front door open wide.

'Thank goodness it's you, sir!' she exclaimed, as we followed Thatcher into the hall. 'I feared it might be the police again, or another of those awful men from the papers. I have sent two of them on their way, this very morning!'

'There, there, Mrs Clarridge,' our client assured her. 'You may put your broom away. These men are friends — Sherlock Holmes and Dr Watson. Mr Holmes is a detective, who I hope will find the truth of this terrible business.'

'Amen to that,' the woman concurred. 'This affair has worn me down more than I'd care to admit.'

'And what is your opinion of this

matter, Mrs Clarridge?' Sherlock Holmes enquired. 'Do you believe your master has run off with Miss Lowell?'

'I do not!' the housekeeper bristled. 'Only — '

Distress showed plainly in her face. 'I don't know what to think,' she continued, gathering her apron in her hands. 'I know I saw him leave. And yet — well, sir, I know there must be some good reason for his actions. Professor Thatcher has always been a kind and decent man. I only hope that will be proved, when all comes to light.'

'I see. Then might I ask you a few questions? Your testimony, I'm sure, will be of great assistance.'

'But of course, sir. I shall help in any way I can.'

'Good. Then tell me, if you would, everything that happened on the night Professor Thatcher disappeared.'

'We had a frightful storm that night, Mr Holmes. Thunder shook the house, and the rain came down in sheets. Professor Thatcher had just finished dinner, and retired to the study. I had started to clear the dishes, when suddenly he returned, wearing his coat and hat and carrying a large umbrella. 'Something important has come up, Mrs Clarridge,' he said. 'I must go out for a bit. Don't worry, I won't be late.' And out he went, without another word, into the night.'

'What of his manner? Did he seem upset?'

'Well, yes, sir. Agitated, sort of. As if something was preying on his mind.'

'Go on.'

'Well, needless to say, I was quite surprised, considering the state of the weather. Friday being my night off, I had planned to go out myself. I enjoy the theatre, and the University Company was doing *HMS Pinafore* at Bishop's Cottage. But with it raining cats and dogs, I decided to stay in. I finished the dishes, and retired to my room to read.'

'And where is your room located?'

'There, sir,' the woman said, pointing to a door at the end of the hall, 'just beside the stairs. The dining room and kitchen are on the left, the study and morning room on the right.'

'Thank you, Mrs Clarridge. One moment, if you please.'

Holmes strode to the door of the housekeeper's room, opened it and stepped inside, then turned back towards us and gazed about the hall. He was, I knew, attempting to put himself in the housekeeper's place.

'From here, you have an unobstructed view, not only of the staircase, but the hallway and front door as well,' he remarked. 'And where is Professor Thatcher's room?'

'At the top of the stairs, sir. The first door on the right. If you step out into the hall a bit, you can see it easily.'

'Quite so,' Holmes murmured, as he did so. He then closed the door and rejoined us. 'Pray continue, Mrs Clarridge.'

'Shortly before nine o'clock, I heard Professor Thatcher return. I remember the time exactly, as I had just put down my book and was preparing myself for bed. Since it was still pouring, I thought the professor might have need of a toddy, or wish me to dry some of his things. So I climbed out of bed, threw on my robe, and went to the door, as I could hear him on the stairs.

'When I stepped out, I was surprised to see the hallway dark, save for one small candle upon the lampstand near the front door. The professor's umbrella stood next to it, but his coat and hat were not upon the rack. Looking up, I could see light from his bedroom, as the door was slightly ajar. I called out to him, and asked if there was anything he needed. 'No,' he replied. 'Nothing, thank you.' So I closed my door and went back to bed.

'I had almost dropped off, when I heard footsteps again, this time descending the stairs. For some reason, Mr Holmes, I suddenly felt something was very wrong. Quick as I could, I lit a lamp and eased open my door, just enough so as to peep out into the hall — '

'And what did you see?' Holmes asked. 'Pray, be precise.'

'Why, there, Lord help me, was Professor Thatcher! He was standing at the front door in his coat and hat, with a bag in his hand! I started to cry out, but before I could utter a sound, he'd pinched the candle and was gone.'

'You are certain it was Professor Thatcher?' I enquired. 'You saw his face?'

'Not exactly, sir. It was dark, and his back was to me, you see. But I'm sure it was the professor. I recognised his hat and coat, and I've packed that brown valise of his a hundred times, if ever I've done it once.'

The old woman gave us a bewildered look. 'Pardon me for saying it, sir,' she added, 'but when you look at it straight, that just doesn't make sense. I mean, who else would be in the professor's bedroom, packing his clothes, if not the professor himself? And as to the door, outside of myself, he has the only key.'

Holmes put a finger to his chin. 'Yes,' he replied. 'Who else, indeed? Continue, Mrs Clarridge. What happened next?'

'For a moment, I didn't quite know what to do, I was so taken aback. Then I grabbed my dressing-gown and hurried out, and went to this side window here, to see what I could see.'

'Which was?'

'Professor Thatcher, sir, just going out to the gate. His head was bent and the rain was whipping at his coat tails, and in the glow of the street lamp, I could see a carriage waiting. When he reached it, he handed up his bag, took the driver's seat, and off he went.'

Holmes and I exchanged glances.

'He drove the cab, you say?'

'Yes, sir. I thought that odd myself.'

'For a university professor, odd indeed. And what type was it? Hansom or four-wheeler?'

'Oh, it was a growler, sir. Of that I'm sure.'

'You said he handed up his bag. Someone else was inside the carriage, then?'

'Well, yes, sir — ' For the first time, the small woman's dark eyes looked away.

'Come, come!' Holmes demanded. 'Tell us all.'

'It was a woman,' the housekeeper replied.

'Miss Lowell?'

'I couldn't say, sir. All I saw was her gloved hand and the sleeve of her dress, as she took the professor's valise.'

'And what colour was this glove and sleeve?'

'I really couldn't say, again, sir. Except that the material was dark rather than light.'

My companion frowned. 'One final point, then,' he continued, 'about the message Professor Thatcher received on Thursday, the day before he disappeared. It did arrive at precisely half past three?'

'Yes, sir. An hour before the professor returned from classes. I left it on his desk in the study.'

'And how would you describe the man who delivered it?'

'He was a tall man, sir. About the same height as the professor, I'd say. And he had dark hair and thick moustaches.'

'Do you recall anything else about him? A scar, perhaps? A limp, a mannerism?'

Mrs Clarridge thought a few seconds, then shook her head. 'No, Mr Holmes. Nothing else, I'm afraid. You see, I had no cause to take further note of him. Messages are delivered here quite commonly.'

'I understand. Thank you, Mrs Clarridge. Your help has been considerable. And now, Mr Thatcher: might I examine your brother's bedroom, and then the study?'

'Of course. Though I doubt if you'll find anything enlightening. The police, you realise, have already searched both rooms quite thoroughly.'

Holmes made a long face. 'If I find nothing, Mr Thatcher,' he said, as we began to climb the stairs, 'that most certainly will be the reason. The police, I have often found, obliterate as much as they discover. Since we hold so few threads at present, I hope, in this instance, that has not been the case.'

Holmes's words, unfortunately, proved to be prophetic, in spite of his meticulous search of Professor Thatcher's sleeping quarters. For a quarter-hour, he crawled and darted nimbly about the room, examining every object — the four-poster bed and nightstand, the dressing table and window sills, a large chest of drawers, even the carpeting and the floorboards. As he put away his glass, however, defeat and frustration showed clearly in his face.

'As I feared,' he exclaimed, 'the police have trampled through like a herd of elephants! The only things undisturbed, it seems, are some large tufts of dust under the professor's bed.'

'Dust?' I queried.

'Yes. Mrs Clarridge, apparently, has been so upset that she has neglected her weekend cleaning.'

Holmes strode to the centre of the room. 'I suspect that our friend Square-toe was here,' he said. 'A loose shoe nail has snagged the carpet in no fewer than three places. Yet it is impossible to tell; the traffic has been too heavy. Cigar ash is pressed into the carpet, as well, and a cigarette stub lies in the tray. But from whose hand did they come? Square-toe, Professor Thatcher, or an inquisitive inspector, as he roamed restlessly about? Remind me, Watson, never again to complain of Lestrade or his minions. Compared to this, they are tidy as household cats.'

'Of one thing, you may be sure,' Jonathon Thatcher stated. 'Neither cigar nor cigarette was smoked here by my brother. A pipe is his only vice.'

'That, and the fact some clothes and toilet articles are missing, seem to be the summation of our findings,' Holmes muttered, as he knelt before the closet. 'But, hello! — What have we here?'

He brought out a pair of slippers, which he proceeded to examine intently. 'These are your brother's?' he asked.

'They are,' the other confirmed. 'Why do you ask?'

'Because I observe that they are not only well-worn, but decidedly expensive. Soft leather, well-stitched, and lined with lamb's wool, which is heavily matted from frequent use.' Holmes smiled. 'Yes. I'll wager these cost one and six, if they cost a farthing.'

'Your appraisal is quite accurate,' Thatcher stated. 'I should know; the slippers were a gift from me, on Christmas last. As I told you before, Aubrey was never a handy man. He chopped off a toe, when he was seven, trying to cut wood. He's not taken well to dampness ever since.'

Holmes fairly beamed, as he heard the words. In his eyes, I noted, was a look I had seen many times before, when the facts of a case were falling into place, though for the life of me, I couldn't fathom why. It was a good time, I decided, to see how much he would reveal.

'Holmes, what are you driving at?' I chided. 'A pair of slippers? What kind of clue is that?'

'The very best kind, Watson,' he answered. 'A clue not even the clumsiest of policemen can erase.' Refusing to say more, he turned to Thatcher, then added, 'Along those lines, I suggest we proceed to the study.'

Upon entering the room, Holmes walked directly to the mantle above the fireplace, directing his attention to a mahogany rack filled with pipes, and a glass humidor of tobacco. As we joined him, I noted a framed picture on the shelf as well, of two men standing beside a large gazebo in the bright sun. The shorter of the two, I recognised immediately, was Jonathon Thatcher.

'Your brother?' I asked, indicating the other man in the photo.

'Yes, that is Aubrey,' Thatcher confirmed. 'The picture was taken last summer, at a picnic on the museum grounds at Elvet Hill.'

'He is much taller than you,' I commented.

'A full head taller, Dr Watson. Facially, we both resemble our dear mother, but it was Aubrey who inherited our father's height. And, as you can see by his moustaches, his coal black hair as well.'

While we conversed, Holmes had been removing the pipes from the rack and examining them, one by one. 'A Dublin with a Cutty stem,' he remarked, as he replaced the one nearest to him. 'And a calabash and a briar, as well — '

'The dark Meerschaum is his favourite,' Thatcher interjected.

'So I gathered,' Holmes replied. 'The colour of the bowl says as much.'

Holmes took down the humidor, extracted some tobacco, and held a pinch of the dark leaf beneath his nose, rubbing it gently between his index finger and thumb. 'Rat trays, without a doubt,' he stated. 'A Turkish blend.'

'Right you are!' cried Thatcher, who was obviously impressed. 'You know your tobaccos, Mr Holmes.'

'It is one of many things of which I've made a study,' my friend explained. 'Your brother had this specially prepared, I take it?'

'Yes. It came from a small shop called the Tin Box, located on Mosley Road. He has smoked nothing else, for as long as I can remember.'

'Another point in our favour, since the jar is full and his pouch still rests upon the shelf. One other question: where did your brother normally keep his revolver?'

'In one of the side drawers of his desk. Which, I can't recall. But if you check, I'm sure you'll find a box of cartridges.'

'And who, besides yourself, might also have known where it was kept?'

'Well — Mrs Clarridge, most certainly.'

'And Miss Lowell?'

'Perhaps. I cannot be positive. You think she is involved, then?'

Holmes drew out his pipe, and began

to fill the bowl from the glass humidor on the mantle. His features were set; his dark eyes gleaming. 'I am as sure of it as I am of your brother's innocence,' he declared. 'For her to be blameless, I must believe that a man of your brother's inexperience could handle a team on a stormy night; or that, knowing he was never to return, still left his favourite pipe and expensive slippers behind.'

Holmes struck a match and inhaled. 'No, no,' he added, shaking his head. 'I do not believe it, in either case.'

While I did not doubt my friend's sincerity, I could not help but feel alarm that he put so much faith in what, it seemed to me, were trifles. The preponderance of facts still pointed to Aubrey Thatcher as a man being blackmailed, a man who had committed murder, and who then absconded with his wife-to-be in order to escape punishment. Despite my misgivings, however, I decided to remain silent until a more suitable moment. Holmes, as oft was his nature, was not ready to tell all. And any protestations from me, I knew, would have only further distressed our client.

Holmes decided that we should go next to University Library, for a talk with Thomas Feeny, after which we would visit the police, since the incriminating documents were in their possession. Thatcher, however, firmly refused to accompany us.

'I have nothing to discuss with Mr Feeny,' he told us. 'Nor do I care to listen to Inspector Doyle, or any of his associates. I have heard quite enough of their theories in recent days.'

All things considered, I could easily understand the poor man's feelings. Before leaving, however, we asked directions to Feeny's office, and secured the address of the Durham police station, which Thatcher said was located on the city's east end, near the Assizes on old Court Lane.

Moments later, we were strolling briskly along in the sunshine across Palace Green, towards the huge grey pillars of University Library which lay ahead. Since we were alone, I decided the time was right to question Holmes on his feelings in the case; my curiosity was as brimming as the sun was bright.

'You know, Holmes, we have come across cases where the party in question was actually guilty,' I reminded him. 'The Boating Lake matter in Regent's Park, for example. Why, Lady Pembrooke deliberately sought your help, in order to throw everyone off the track.'

'I do recall the case, Watson.'

'Well, it does seem to me that we're grasping at straws in this. Pipes and slippers, indeed! The one concrete thing we have discovered is the evidence of the square-toed shoes. And they prove conclusively that Aubrey Thatcher was at the scene of the murder, that he returned home, packed a bag and left again in flight.'

'And what if they are not his shoes?'

'Now that is impossible, surely.'

Holmes paused, a bemused look upon his face. 'Is it? Of the six pairs I examined in his closet, not one was of that fashion. Then, too, there is the matter of the gun.'

'What of it? There seems no question as to whom it did belong.'

'The question, Watson, is who knew

that the gun was kept in Aubrey Thatcher's desk. Is it too much to suppose, for example, that in six months' time Miss Lowell had not discovered it? For all we know, Thatcher may have shown it to her himself, for whatever reason.'

'My dear Holmes, you must enlighten me,' I rejoined. 'I may be very stupid, but I haven't the faintest idea what you're getting at.'

With a sigh, Holmes placed a reassuring hand upon my shoulder. 'It is a perplexing business, I do admit,' he said. 'Just when I catch a glimpse of light, the darkness rolls in again. What is most damning is that almost all the facts seem to point in one direction, while my instincts point the other.'

'And what do your instincts say?'

'That Aubrey Thatcher is innocent. And that this is a far more devious, more sinister affair than the police suspect. From the very start of this case, Watson, little warning bells have been going off inside my mind.'

'Bells?'

'Yes. The first was at the station, when Jonathon Thatcher told us of his brother's alleged indiscretion, and that he had indeed withdrawn five thousand pounds before he fled. Given Thatcher's innocence, blackmail by Samuelson was obvious — and forgery was strongly suggested.'

'Forgery?'

'Of course. How else does a document come to have two different authors, ten years apart?'

'But why would Thatcher consent to paying, if he had committed no crime?'

'That is the most terrifying thing about blackmail, Watson. In most cases an innocent victim is afraid to fight the accusation, no matter how false. For once it becomes public, a name is smeared, a reputation brought into question, no matter what the final outcome. Thatcher, too, remember, had Miss Lowell to consider: would she marry a man whose station was so beleaguered?'

'Come, come, Holmes. For this to be true, you're asking me to believe that a simple file clerk was not only a blackmailer, but a forger as well.'

'Perhaps I am. That's where the second bell comes in. It sounded, strong and clear, when we were riding in the carriage with Jonathon Thatcher, and I asked him about his feelings towards Miss Lowell. I don't suppose you recall the name, Arnold Saxby?'

'Saxby, Saxby . . . But, of course! The Western securities scandal, two years ago.'

'Correct. Arnold Saxby, a master forger, with a decided bent towards blackmail. That he was guilty, I have no doubt, yet he was acquitted for lack of evidence. After which, he dropped out of sight, and has not been heard of since.'

'But what has he to do with this case?'

'Arnold Saxby,' Holmes said, 'was a tall man, with dark moustaches.'

'Good Lord! The messenger at Mrs Clarridge's door!'

'Presumably. And much more than that, Watson, if my theory proves correct. At any rate, Saxby was not the only person indicted in the Western affair. Also charged, and acquitted, was his common-law wife, Annie Langford.' Holmes paused, then added, 'She had a passion for the colour blue.'

For a moment I felt short of breath, as though someone had struck my chest a heavy blow. A chill passed through me that not even the warmth of the afternoon sun could erase. 'But Holmes, this is incredible!' I gasped. 'Why, A.S. and A.L.! Even the initials match!'

Holmes cast me a rueful glance. 'And yet, for all I know, I am not halfway home to offering a solution, much less proving it,' he admitted. 'My case is built, almost entirely, upon coincidence, nuance, suspicion. And that, my dear fellow, is the loudest bell of all, which keeps jangling away in my brain. The singular, almost unique nature of this case.'

'Whatever do you mean?'

'Think, Watson! How many times have we seen it before? A crime is planned, a deception carried out, the perpetrators are suspected. And yet, upon close examination, it is nigh impossible to connect them to the act itself. I know of only one man who excels at such disassociation, such muddying of the waters. He was the man, two years ago, whose mechanisations so successfully shielded Saxby. And who, until January last, held a professorship in mathematics at this very university.'

'My God! Moriarty!'

'None other, Watson. Professor James Moriarty, the master schemer. Even here, so far from London, the brushstrokes of his insidious technique are impossible to miss. This affair bears his trademark as if it were stamped in wax.'

Behind us, the bells of the Lady Chapel resonantly tolled the hour, as if to underscore the words my friend had uttered. It was at that very moment that I suddenly felt certain he was upon the right track, the facts of the case notwithstanding.

'Well, if Moriarty and Thatcher both taught in the same department, it's likely they came in contact,' I ventured. 'Might they have had a falling out of some sort, for whatever reason?'

'It is quite possible, Watson. We do know Moriarty left here under some sort of cloud in January. Thatcher, you recall, first met Annie Lowell — nay, Langford — shortly after. I would not be surprised if it were about the same time that Arnold Samuelson — or Saxby, as we may call him — secured his position at University Library.'

'Why, then it's clear as day! The two were hired by Moriarty to blackmail Aubrey Thatcher from the start!'

'My thoughts, exactly. Yet Saxby now lies dead in the morgue, and the professor and Annie Langford have fled.'

'By his picture, Thatcher seemed a handsome chap. And he does possess money and position. Might the woman have thrown Saxby over?'

'If so,' Sherlock Holmes said, 'then heaven help them. Moriarty's rule is strict; there is but one punishment for those who cross him. If Thatcher and Annie Langford left Saxby on the tracks, they are not merely fleeing from the law. They are fleeing for their lives!'

Our conversation with Thomas Feeny yielded little in the way of new information. However, he did confirm the details of his meeting with Samuelson just hours before his death, and his physical description of the man matched that of the messenger at Mrs Clarridge's door. Samuelson, Feeny said, had been employed the third week in February, filling a vacancy which had been open several weeks. He had come highly recommended, with letters from Oxford and Maynooth, and was from the start a diligent and hard-working employee, putting in long hours to help update the library's new cross-indexing system in July. It was then, Samuelson told him, that he had stumbled upon the fact that Professor Thatcher's doctoral thesis was nearly identical to one written by one William Booker, who had himself graduated nearly a decade before.

'You inspected the documents yourself?' Holmes asked.

'I did,' the librarian replied. 'Save for a brief introduction, they were the same.'

'And how did you identify the body? I understand it was . . . quite mutilated.'

'Quite. My identification was based on Samuelson's clothing, and his signet ring.

The police also found his wallet near the tracks, I'm told.'

'Ah, you did not view it then?'

'Only briefly. Frankly, there was not much to see. The head and shoulders had been horribly disfigured. I was, however, able to discern the dark colour of Samuelson's hair, and his full moustaches.'

'Well, then it all seems certain,' Holmes remarked, as he rose to leave. 'One other point: did Samuelson smoke a pipe?'

'He did. A Dublin, as I recall. I never knew him to be without it.'

My companion smiled. 'Is that so? Well, well. Thank you for your time, Mr Feeny. You have been very helpful indeed. Good day.'

Once outside, Holmes hailed a passing hansom, and directed the driver to convey us to the headquarters of the police, giving him the address which Thatcher had supplied.

'Feeny certainly told us little,' I commented, as we clattered off.

'On the contrary, Watson. I am now certain Moriarty knew of the vacancy on

Feeny's staff. It had been open for some time, remember. What better way to put his man in contact with the very documents he so desired? Saxby, no doubt, did much of the work at the library itself, on the nights he chose to stay late.'

'But shouldn't we have asked to see the letters of recommendation?' I suggested. 'They might be forgeries as well.'

'To what end, Watson? Either the letters are forged, or the real Arnold Samuelson is no longer of this world. Deceased, I would guess, sometime in February or early March. By now, the question is immaterial, in any case.'

Shortly after, our cab deposited us at the steps of the Durham police station, located within a stone's throw of both the Assizes and Her Majesty's Prison. Once inside, Holmes identified himself to a burly sergeant at the front desk, and moments later we found ourselves ushered into the office of Montgomery Doyle, head of Durham's detective force. Doyle was a balding man of average height, with bushy eyebrows and a sandy-coloured moustache. His impassive face and humourless eyes bore the stamp of his profession, and he carried the stern bearing of a man who is accustomed to wielding authority.

'Good afternoon, Mr Holmes,' Doyle said, as he rose from his desk to greet us. 'And this must be Dr Watson.'

'Glad to meet you,' I said, as we all shook hands.

Doyle motioned us to some chairs. 'Sit down, then, gentlemen, and tell me how I can be of service. You are investigating the murder by Aubrey Thatcher, I take it. Why else would London's most famous detective be traversing about the Wear?'

'You are correct,' my friend confirmed. 'I have been employed by his brother, Jonathon, only this very morning.'

'Ah, yes, the brother. Understandable, of course. But I think he has misled you; this is not a difficult case. The findings of the coroner's jury are quite conclusive. All that remains is to apprehend the professor, in order to begin proceedings.'

'Your theory in the matter, then?'

'There is no theory to it. We can prove

conclusively that Aubrey Thatcher shot Arnold Samuelson, threw his body on the tracks, and fled with this woman, Annie Lowell. Blackmail was the motive, and the murder weapon was his own.'

'What you say may all be true,' Holmes rejoined, a bit coolly. 'Still, I should like to see the evidence at hand.'

'Then see it you shall,' the other declared. 'I'm not a short-sighted man, sir. I am aware of some of your previous efforts on behalf of the force. I only hate to see you waste your time. Mark my words: Jack Ketch will have Aubrey Thatcher, once he's apprehended.'

Doyle rose, and led us across the room to a wooden table, upon which lay two expensively-bound volumes, a revolver, a spent bullet and some papers — one of which I perceived to be the original of the note Jonathon Thatcher had shown us at the station.

'It's plain enough to see,' the chief explained. 'Booker's thesis is on the left, Thatcher's on the right. The revolver has been identified by his brother, and this is the slug that was removed from the body.'

'And these?' I asked, indicating the papers.

'This letter was taken from Thatcher's desk; it matches the handwriting of his thesis. The library employment card does as much for Samuelson's note, which was delivered to Thatcher's house. And this,' he added, significantly, 'is Thatcher's account book, showing a withdrawal of five thousand pounds the day before he fled. More than enough evidence to hang a man, I'd say.'

Holmes opened both books to where they had been marked, and began to quickly flip through the pages.

'We have read them quite thoroughly, Mr Holmes,' the policeman remarked. 'There is no doubt they are the same.'

'What is the subject?' I enquired.

'The treatise is titled, 'Plane Co-ordinate Geometry and Conic Sections',' Doyle replied. 'It deals with the transformation of co-ordinates, or so I'm told. Frankly, I found it rather heavy going.'

As we talked, I noted Holmes had closed both books and continued to inspect them intently, first running his glass along the edges of the pages from top to bottom, and then from the front to the base of the spine. After which, he re-opened each volume wide and held it to the light, examining the binding closely.

'You have considered forgery?' Holmes asked, at last.

'Most certainly,' the other declared. 'Our expert, however, insists both letter and thesis are in Aubrey Thatcher's hand.'

'Of that, I had no doubt,' Holmes said. 'It was to Booker's thesis I was referring.'

Doyle appeared struck. For an instant, he glanced first at Holmes and then myself, seemingly unable to speak. 'I am afraid I do not follow you, sir,' he said, finally. 'Your suggestion, frankly, strikes me as incredible! It does not fit the facts.'

'And yet, clearly, it has been done,' Holmes persisted.

'How can you tell?'

'By comparing the glue along the bindings. Such glue darkens as it ages. Yet, as you can see by the glass, the glue on Booker's volume is decidedly lighter in colour.'

'Which means the book has been rebound!' I cried.

'Precisely, Watson. Note, too, the edge of the pages. When the book is closed, a faint, almost undetectable line appears — newer paper, certainly, though an able attempt has been made to age it, probably by rubbing it with dust. A masterful job! Yet the traces remain, none the less.'

'You seem to have a point,' Doyle admitted, as he peered through Holmes's glass. 'But the boards themselves seem rightly aged.'

'And so they are. I'll wager you could search University Library for a year, and not find the book from which they were stolen.'

The dour policeman pondered for a moment, a look of consternation upon his face. 'If what you say is true, what is the motive then?'

'To falsely incriminate Professor Aubrey Thatcher. That, Inspector, is what lies at the heart of this matter. Hah! The cleverness of it all. Rather than changing Thatcher's manuscript to match another, another was merely changed to tally with his.'

'And who, might I ask, was responsible

for this changing?'

'Arnold Saxby, one of the most skilful forgers in all of England. Since February he has resided here — known as Arnold Samuelson.'

'What?'

'It is also no coincidence,' Holmes continued, 'that his common-law wife has been here as well. Her name is Annie Langford, a surname she has recently exchanged for Lowell.'

Doyle mulled this over for a moment. 'You can prove it?' he asked, sternly.

'No, but you can, if you wire Inspector Lestrade at Scotland Yard for all the particulars. I daresay a complete dossier, including pictures, should arrive within a day.'

A satisfied look crossed the policeman's face. 'Then you have done me no small service, Mr Holmes,' he said, with just a hint of gratification. 'If what you say is true, this case was certainly not merely blackmail, but an affair of the heart as well! The woman turned Saxby over, I'd say, just when his plot was about to hatch.'

Holmes looked dismayed. What was it he had told me, about so much being revealed, in order to conceal? Moriarty, it seemed had laid his plans perfectly once again.

'It is, I admit, a theory which deserves consideration,' my friend said, finally, 'though there are a few points I should still care to pursue. Might I ask a favour? The number of Annie Lowell's rooming house and Arnold Samuelson's flat? Also, I would be interested in knowing where Mr Booker now resides.'

'I have both addresses here,' Doyle said, as he walked back to his desk. 'As to Booker, I shall have a constable contact the university. They do, oft-times, keep quite good track of where their people relocate. And you are staying — ?'

'At the Rose and Crown,' I interjected.

Doyle scribbled down the information we sought, then handed it to my friend. 'You'll need this note to gain admittance,' he said, 'since both rooms are still under guard. It is the least I can do, Mr Holmes, after what you have revealed. Your theory clears up some questions I had been weighing.'

Holmes looked upon the man intently. 'There is much more to this than we now know,' he insisted, gravely. 'I feel it in my bones.'

Try as he might, the other could not completely mask his look of scepticism. 'With all regard to your feelings, sir,' he said, 'I think I shall confine myself to following up the facts. I shall wire Scotland Yard at once. Thank you, and good day. And to you, Dr Watson.'

Albert House, where Annie Lowell had roomed, turned out to be a grimy, red-brick structure on Aylsham Row, just off Crossgate, which was clearly struggling to maintain its dignity. Its sign, which bore the monarch's features, had faded noticeably; there was no doorman and the once-white trim of its gutters and windows had long since turned to grey. Inside, at the front desk, we encountered the redoubtable Mrs Purcell, who gruffly sent us up the stairs to Number Four, where a stocky constable stood beside the door. Upon reading Doyle's note, he allowed us to enter, after which Holmes conducted his usual thorough search of the woman's rooms. We then returned to the lobby, where my colleague — after artfully engaging Mrs Purcell in a few moments of light conversation — persuaded the reluctant landlady to recount again for us the events of Friday eve last.

A gold sovereign, it should be noted, was what finally did the trick.

'Her leaving was a shock to me, Lord knows!' the woman declared, with some indignation. 'Why, had the Prince himself walked through those doors, I shouldn't have been more surprised! As I'm sure you both have noticed, this is a first-rate domicile; and Miss Lowell was my best of boarders. Been with us since February, she had! And in all that time, not once did she cause a fuss, and she always paid in advance.'

'She'd mentioned nothing before about leaving, then?' I asked.

'Not a word! It was just before eight that night when she came down, and asked me if I'd call a boy to fetch her things. Cor, I felt like I'd been biffed! It was all I could do to keep my jaw from dropping.'

'What reason did she give for this . . . sudden departure?' Sherlock Holmes asked.

'None at all, that I could see. Oh, she was most apologetic! 'I've no complaint about the establishment,' she said. 'You must understand. An opportunity has presented itself, and I've found preferable lodgings elsewhere through a friend.' A cab, she told me, would be arriving shortly.

'Well, what was I to do? Though I knew her story was much too thin. First off, the hour was odd; then, too, it was raining cats and dogs! 'Very well,' I said, reminding her that our rates were weekly. No matter, she said, she didn't mind; the extra day was mine.'

'And how was she dressed?' Holmes enquired.

'Dressed? Why, smart as always; I'd never seen her otherwise. As I recall, she wore a navy dress that night, with matching cape and gloves.' Mrs Purcell sniffed, and added, 'What a shame. To see her, you'd never think she was no lady.'

As she spoke, I cast a glance in Holmes's direction, recalling Mrs Clarridge's words. The material of the woman's sleeve, she'd told us, had been dark, as opposed to light.

'Proceed,' Holmes said.

'Well, I sent a lad up, and Miss Lowell took a seat right over there,' she said, indicating a small settee. 'About the time he returned with her luggage, I saw a four-wheeler pull up out front.' She paused, giving us both a teasing look. 'And I'll bet this sovereign on a pint, you'll never guess what happened next.'

'Pray, tell us then.'

'Well, as you might expect, the driver hopped down — but he didn't open the carriage door! Walked right in himself, he did, dripping from head to foot!'

Holmes suddenly bolted to attention, like a seasoned hound who has found the scent. 'You are certain it was the driver?' he asked. 'And not the passenger from within?'

Mrs Purcell appeared insulted. 'Strike me down, if it wasn't,' she replied. 'My eyesight is not faulty, and there's a street lamp right outside. And as you can see, if you'd care to turn round, my view is not impeded.'

'Describe this cabbie, then.'

'He was a tall fellow. Lean, with dark moustaches.'

'And wearing a signet ring?'

'Why, yes, now that you mention it. I thought at the time it seemed a bit above his wallet.'

'His suit? It was this colour?' Holmes asked, holding up the scrap of cloth he had found beside the tracks.

'Could be. Close enough, if it wasn't.'

This time, Holmes and I exchanged a glance. My mind was racing. Had it really been Saxby driving the professor's carriage? And, if so, how had it come to happen? While I was unable to form a conclusion, I felt certain we were finally getting at the truth.

'Tell us,' Holmes asked, 'What happened next?'

'Well, he walks over, and asks if she is Miss Annie Lowell, and she said yes. 'Good', he said. 'Professor Thatcher is waiting for you in the carriage; I'll get your things.' And then he comes over to me and asks to settle up, he does! Well, I was dumbfounded: a cabbie asking about a lady's bill! 'She's paid in advance,' I said. 'That's very well', he told me. 'Professor Thatcher made a point that I should ask.' And with that, he grabbed her bags, and out the door they went.'

'You watched them leave?'

'I had nothing else to do. And it was a bit strange, you must admit.'

'So?'

'So I walked over by that flower stand, and saw him throw up her luggage. She was already in the carriage, smiling and talking to someone else.'

'Professor Thatcher?'

'I assume so. I could not be entirely certain, since he was sitting in the shadow. Miss Lowell, however, I saw quite clearly in the street light, in spite of the pouring rain.'

Holmes clapped his hands together, a satisfied look upon his face. 'Thank you, Mrs Purcell!' he cried. 'As sovereigns go, the one I passed to you was worth every shilling. Good day to you, madam! Come along, Watson.'

Once outside, however, my friend's mood darkened. He smacked his fist into his other hand. 'The clever devils!' he muttered. 'Ah, Watson, what a fool I've been!'

'You've solved it, then?'

'I believe I have. Although there are a few minor details which we must confirm.'

Holmes handed me the note Inspector Doyle had given us not an hour before. 'By my watch, it is four o'clock,' he said. 'We will save considerable time, at this point, by going our separate ways. You, Watson, will take a cab to Saxby's flat. There are two items I wish you to search for among his things, and there is a question which must be put to whoever is in charge. You should, I think, have no trouble meeting me back at the Rose and Crown by six.'

'Ah, for dinner, surely.'

Holmes frowned. 'A sandwich, per-haps, if we have time,' he said. 'We must return to the Durham police station by seven.'

'But for what reason?'

'To confer with Inspector Doyle and Professor Cromwell, to put an end to this sinister business. I shall, among other things, send them both messages to that effect.'

'Where are you off to now, then?'

Holmes heaved a sigh of discontent. I could tell he was not pleased with himself at all. 'The morgue, Watson. Had I gone there first, I should have certainly detected Moriarty's scheme much sooner — and saved us several hours of work, as well.'

While I had to admit that I was lost, I could not help but bow my head and purse my lips, at a complete loss. 'Holmes, please!' I implored. 'You cannot leave me in the dark like this! I must have some sort of clue as to what's gone on.'

My companion offered me one of his slight, mysterious smiles. 'We have a cabbie who does a professor's bidding, and a professor who drives a cab,' he said. 'A rather peculiar combination, wouldn't you say? Think along those lines, Watson, and I'm sure you'll have no trouble picking up the thread.'

At which point, Holmes whistled twice at a passing hansom, giving me detailed instructions before he climbed aboard. After signalling my own conveyance, I rode to Saxby's flat on Margey Lane, where I did as I had been instructed, and rejoined Holmes in our rooms at the Rose and Crown, shortly before six-thirty.

I found him stretched out somewhat morosely across our bed, smoking a pipeful of the strongest shag, three open envelopes and their contents by his side.

'It was as you suspected, Holmes,' I told him. 'A Dublin Cutty was nowhere to be found, and all the shoes were square-toed as well. According to the landlord, Samuelson — or that is, Saxby — received very little mail, but all of it was from London, posted from various addresses.'

'Moriarty does not miss a trick,' my friend replied. 'You have deduced what has happened, then?'

'I must confess that I have not,' I answered. 'In spite of the clue which you supplied.'

'Then this, perhaps, will help,' Holmes said, tossing me one of the messages from upon the bed.

Glancing down, I read:

Dear Mr Holmes,

In answer to your question, it was the fourth toe of his left foot. Though to what end it matters, I cannot imagine.

Respectfully,
Jonathon Thatcher

'Holmes,' I asked, even more confused, 'what does this mean?'

'The very worst, I assure you, Watson. It means that while I have solved the case, matters cannot be rectified. We have arrived too late for that. But come, we must be off! It is closing in on seven.'

As we clattered across Durham's busy streets in the growing darkness, Holmes said not a word. Having been at this juncture many times before, I knew it was wise not to press him, since all would be revealed shortly.

At the station, Holmes and I were again shown into the office of Montgomery

Doyle, where we were introduced to Professor Ellis Cromwell, an elderly gentleman whose silver mane, black frock coat and shiny pince-nez made him appear the very picture of a member of the academia.

'I am honoured, Mr Holmes,' Cromwell stated, as the two shook hands. 'However, I am not clear as to what assistance, if any, I can lend in this affair. I received your note, I must admit, with some surprise.'

'As did I,' Doyle interjected, reaching for a cigar. 'You have, I take it, discovered something important, to call us here so hurriedly and at this house.'

'What I have discovered will solve this matter,' Holmes said. 'I have found Professor Aubrey Thatcher.'

'What!' Doyle cried, nearly dropping the match he had just struck. 'Tell us then, man! Where is he?'

'In your own morgue. It was he who was shot and thrown upon the tracks.'

We were all stunned by Holmes's revelation. Observing the pale colour of Professor Cromwell's cheeks, I offered him a chair. Doyle, who was made of sterner stuff, had quickly regained his composure and was carefully lighting his cigar. He then slid behind his desk. 'I must remind you, Mr Holmes,' he said, 'that the body has been positively identified — '

' — by clothes, a signet ring and a wallet. As it was meant to be. It is not coincidence the two men were of the same approximate build, and had the same colour hair. Saxby, I imagine, had to grow a moustache. The trains passing through the night did the rest.'

'What you say is pure conjecture,' the inspector insisted. 'Where is your proof?'

'Here,' Holmes said, handing him the note he had shown me earlier. 'Thatcher chopped off that toe by accident, as a child. When I examined the body, the same toe was missing. I also observed a nasty scar; the point, obviously where the axe, so many years ago, had struck.'

Doyle thought a moment, then sprang up, a look of revelation upon his face. 'By Heaven, sir!' he declared. 'If what you say is true, then it was Saxby, and not the professor, who left town with the woman!'

Holmes clenched his fist in anger, and began to pace. 'Precisely! But not before they had made poor Thatcher victim of one of the most vile conspiracies imaginable! This was no mere killing; it was a calculated revenge of the very worst sort. The plan was to take everything before they fled — his money, his life, even his reputation!'

Doyle appeared impressed by my friend's outburst, and a trifle perplexed. 'Clearly, sir, you know considerably more of this than I,' he admitted, returning to his chair. 'My only goal is that all be brought to light. I should be interested to hear what you think has transpired.'

'The chronology of the affair is simple enough,' Holmes said. 'Saxby and Langford arrived in February; he to secure a job at University Library, she to bring herself in contact with Professor Thatcher. While the hard-working Saxby was forging Booker's thesis to match, she was seducing him with her feminine wiles. For a man of Thatcher's age and inexperience, such a woman's attentions would have been heady stuff, indeed; he found himself smitten, as she had planned.

'During those halcyon months, I have no doubt Langford took great pains to learn the habits of the house — that Mrs Clarridge religiously attended the theatre on Fridays, for example, or that Thatcher kept a revolver in his desk. An impression of the keys, both front and back, was also quite likely made.

'Once Booker's thesis had been replaced, the trap was sprung. Saxby confronted Thatcher, threatening him with exposure unless he paid. At first, the professor probably refused, knowing he had committed no crime. But as his appointment to the Senate — and imminent marriage — drew near, he finally did give in. Who knows the true particulars? Perhaps, finally, he did bare all to Langford, hoping she would stand by him. Her reaction, I'd wager, was anything but reassuring.'

'So he did go to the park that night to pay?' I suggested.

'Yes. What he did not know was that Saxby's motive was much deeper; that he waited with the professor's own gun in his hand.'

Suddenly, it all hit me. 'Good Lord, Holmes!' I cried. 'The square-toed shoes! They, and the testimony of Mrs Purcell, prove it was Saxby who shot Thatcher, then picked up Langford, and returned to the professor's home for his belongings!'

Holmes clapped his hands. 'Capital, Watson! What Mrs Clarridge saw, of course, was Saxby dressed in the professor's hat and coat, hurrying out of the door. They had not counted on her being there, and it nearly upset their plans.'

'But she says she heard him speak.'

'In the thunder and rain, she heard a voice,' Holmes stated. 'Given the circumstances, Watson, had you ever heard Thatcher speak, I daresay even you could have passed off an imitation.'

The inspector took a long draw on his cigar. 'You seem to have explained it all very well, Mr Holmes,' he concurred, at length. 'Except one thing, and that is motive. Who would want to so ruin a man?'

'Professor Cromwell, I'm sure, can answer that,' Holmes said, 'since you refer to a man, who until January of this year, taught at this very university — '

The old man gasped.

' — and who, at this very moment, sits in London at the head of a criminal organisation more vast, more powerful, than the world has ever seen.'

'Moriarty! James Moriarty!' Cromwell cried, clearly shaken. 'God help me, then! Thatcher's death is upon my conscience. I should have made him pay!'

'Moriarty?' Doyle queried. 'I have never heard the name. Who is this villain, then?'

Cromwell shook his head sadly. Even though the old gentleman was seated, I could see he was leaning heavily upon his stick for more support. 'He is a man of outstanding intellectual gifts,' Cromwell said. 'Have you read his theory, 'Dynamics of an Asteroid'? Some argue he owes a debt to Dodgson, but I cannot agree. He is the visionary of our decade.

'Until this January last, I felt Professor Moriarty had a most brilliant academic career ahead of him. My only concern was that another, larger, institution might lure him from us. It was then I learned of his darker side.'

'From Professor Aubrey Thatcher?' Holmes suggested.

Cromwell nodded. 'Aubrey was not a theorist,' he said, 'but he was a sound instructor, honest and diligent. Upon discovering that Moriarty had been diverting certain departmental funds to his own ends, he did not hesitate to bring the matter before me.

'It was no easy choice for me, gentlemen. Moriarty was the brightest star upon our horizon; yet I also realised that if I refused to act, all that I and the university stand for would have become a sham. So I offered Moriarty a choice: leave the university, or face prosecution for the monies he had squandered. As you are well aware, Mr Holmes, he left — '

' — but did not forget! In fact, no sooner had Moriarty established himself in London, than he began to plot his insidious revenge. Not only would he repay Thatcher in kind — dishonouring his name and forcing him from the university — but he would take his life, as well!' Holmes paused a moment, placing a finger to his lips. 'His wrath, I feel certain, was further fuelled by your announcement of Thatcher's appointment to the Senate,' he added. 'After all, he and you alone knew what high service Thatcher had rendered the university.'

'I sense you are correct, Mr Holmes,' Cromwell agreed. 'But in spite of all that has transpired, I do not regret the choice. Aubrey Thatcher's loyalty to Durham remains unquestioned.'

Once again, Montgomery Doyle was on his feet. 'This is a heinous crime,' he said. 'Rest assured, gentlemen. I shall alert Scotland Yard, and the Port Authority, immediately! Warrants shall be drawn — for the two who fled, and this Moriarty fellow, as well!'

Holmes shook his head. 'Saxby and Langford you may apprehend,' he said. 'If so, the chances of a conviction seem fair. But I guarantee you, Inspector, when it comes to Moriarty, no connection to any of this shall ever be convincingly made.'

Doyle appeared annoyed. 'You seem quite certain on that point, sir,' he replied, coolly. 'I prefer to think that Moriarty must answer to British law.'

'The trick,' Holmes told him, 'is to place him in the dock. Believe me, Inspector, I know his ways! His alibi, for the weekend past, shall be as strong as Dover's cliffs; Saxby and Langford, if caught, will deny any knowledge of the man. And if you're lucky enough to discover correspondence, not a sheet of it will be signed.' Holmes laughed. 'Why, marrying Watson into Buckingham Palace would be child's play, compared to linking Moriarty to Thatcher's death!'

Doyle frowned. 'You seem sure of your facts,' he conceded. 'However, I shall ask Scotland Yard's advice; should it concur with yours, then Saxby and Langford will be our prey. If not, I shall travel south, place the darbies on Moriarty's wrists myself, and force him to prove his story.'

'As you wish. And now, gentlemen, if you will excuse us, Watson and I must go. We have one final task to perform this night, before we've earned our beds. Our client must be informed of this sad turn of events.'

Though our errand was a heavy one, I none the less welcomed the chance for a few moments alone with my friend, once we had hailed a cab and clattered off into the night. There were a number of questions I wished to press.

'Holmes,' I asked, as we rode along, 'when did you first suspect that it was Thatcher, and not Saxby, who had been killed?'

'At the professor's house, when Mrs Clarridge told her story. It occurred to me that she had not actually seen his face. Then, too, there were no square-toed shoes in Thatcher's closet. Yet, Square-toe had surely been there; you recall the footprint in the clay? Most convincing, however, was the fact his slippers remained, and that his pipe lay on the rack.'

'That seems like pretty shaky ground to me.'

'How many times have I told you, Watson, that the smallest point may often be the most essential? Barring fire or earthquake, no Englishman would leave his favourite pipe behind. Was there a Dublin lying about in Saxby's rooms? I rest my case.'

'Still, you couldn't be sure. Not until you'd visited the morgue, at any rate.'

'Correct. I should have done it sooner, but I failed to recognise what an important clue Jonathon Thatcher had inadvertently given us. I was, I admit, too caught up in theories of cross and doublecross. Reveal to conceal, remember?'

'But you were right. That is exactly what Moriarty did.'

'And a clever show it was. Performed admirably, especially by Annie Langford, chatting happily to no one as she sat in Saxby's cab.'

'I see now what you were driving at. There should have been a coachman at the professor's house, since there was one at the hotel.'

'And there should have been a professor, Watson. Instead, there was only a cabbie matching Saxby's description, wearing Saxby's clothes. And a tall man in the professor's coat and hat, hurrying off with his luggage into the night.'

'Good Lord, Holmes! A thought just hit me. If Saxby was still wearing his original suit when he picked up Annie Langford, then Aubrey Thatcher's body must have been inside the cab!'

'It is quite likely. A pair as cold-blooded as they could certainly pull it off. From the Prince Albert, I imagine, they returned to the safe remoteness of the park, where clothes were switched and the body was dumped on the tracks. Saxby needed the professor's garments, after all, for his part in the charade.'

'And what of the five thousand pounds, Holmes? Will Moriarty get that, as well?'

'We have no way of knowing, Watson. I suspect, however, that it was Saxby and Langford's commission — along with tickets to the Continent.'

'Do you think the police will apprehend them?'

'Perhaps. Though I'm sure their escape route has been well planned.' Holmes smacked his fist into his hand, and uttered a curse of frustration into the night. 'Mark my words, Watson,' he vowed. 'Some day, I shall bring this devil to account!'

For a few moments, we bumped along in silence, as houses and street lamps passed by outside.

'Watson,' Holmes said. 'Are you still game to view the cathedral tomorrow?'

'I should like that very much.'

'Good. Then we shall rise early, and spend some reflective hours strolling about its transepts, before we return to London. Ah, but our cab is slowing! Are we there already? . . . The lights are burning; he's home, then. Poor man! I only wish that we had better news to convey.'

★   ★   ★

A postscript must be added to this case. Saxby and Langford were never apprehended by the police. While it was generally assumed they had fled to Europe, the New York Port Authority was also wired particulars; nothing ever came of it. Six months later, a report reached us that the two had died in a train crash near Tours, but it was never confirmed. Over the years, they never resurfaced, and what has become of them remains a mystery to this day.

The Case of the Baffled Courier

We had been back at Baker Street little more than a week when the spectre of Moriarty rose before us again.

The Tuesday to which I now refer was an unseasonably bitter day. Blustery winds swirled through the cobblestone streets and about the gabled housetops of London, while dark grey clouds promised rain. Overnight, the weather had turned cold, bringing with it that first unwelcome hint of impending winter, which causes even the hardiest of souls to immediately bring out again his ulster and cravat.

Seduced by the blanketed warmth of my bed, I slept late. Upon rising a little before nine, I hurried down to find my companion, Sherlock Holmes, already dressed and busily engaged at his desk with gluepot and scissors, clipping items of interest for his scrapbook from the dailies which Mrs Hudson had saved in our absence. A scrap of toast upon his plate showed that he had long ago partaken of breakfast. Alas, I found, the porridge had also grown quite cold.

'Released from the spell of Morpheus at last, I see,' Holmes said, as I poured myself a steaming cup of coffee. 'It is just as well; I was about to wake you.'

'Is that so?'

'Yes. I should like your assistance shortly, unless you have other plans.'

Turning my chair closer to the crackling fire, I sank down, and placed my slippered feet upon the fender. 'Consider me at your disposal, then,' I told him, after a warming sip from my cup. 'I had thought to start my day by reading Guy Boothby's latest, but that can surely wait.'

'Excellent! Then you shall be my faithful Boswell once again, with pen and notebook ready in hand.'

'Ah, you have a client?'

Holmes nodded, a gleam in his gimlet eyes. Rising, he brought me a small sheet of embossed notepaper, which, he said, had been delivered not an hour before. Upon it was written the following:

My dear Mr Holmes,

I have been referred to you by a mutual acquaintance, Dr Percy Trevelyan, who insists you are the only man fit to advise me on a perplexing matter which I have been engaged to undertake. I shall take the liberty of calling this morning, shortly after nine.

Respectfully,
Howard Montclair

'Trevelyan!' I cried. 'Why, he was the fellow who put us on to the Worthingdon bank gang![1] Good Lord, Holmes, I wonder who is this Howard Montclair?'

'He is a solicitor, Watson. Note the trademark on the stationery.'

'H'mm. Merryweather & Stone. A quite respected firm.'

'Indeed. It is rather unusual, you must admit. A man who is paid generously to

[1] *The Case of the Resident Patient*, October 6–7, 1887.

114

give legal counsel, seeking my advice?'
Holmes strode to the window above his
desk, and glanced down in the street. 'Ah!
A cab is at the kerb, I see. That must be
him. Fetch your notebook, Doctor. His
story may not be so adventurous as your
sixpenny novel, but I have no doubt it
should prove interesting.'

No sooner had I done so than we heard
the clattering ring of our front bell, and
Mrs Hudson's voice below. Footsteps
followed upon the stairs, and a singular
knock at the door, as she ushered in our
guest.

Howard Montclair was a distinguished-
looking fellow of about middle age, of
medium height and weight. He had a
wide, honest countenance, a no-nonsense
air, and a full head of the darkest brown
hair, whose sideburns had begun to grey.
His heavy brown Chesterfield, gloves and
matching topper, I felt, were suitable for
the weather, and I also noticed, as we
were introduced, that a black armband
hung from his left sleeve, denoting that he
was in mourning.

'You have our deepest sympathies,'

Holmes told him, as I took his outer attire. 'A relative, I presume?'

'You are correct,' Montclair stated. 'It has been two weeks since I lost my younger brother, Arthur. A skiing accident in the Alps.'

'He was on vacation there?' I asked.

'No. Arthur was with the diplomatic corps in Rome. A stenographer, assigned to Sir William Morrison at the consulate since August. He lived with the Morrisons at their villa, outside the city. From what I'm told, Arthur had only recently taken up the sport. He went up the mountain and never came down. They have not yet found his body.'

'How horrible!' I rejoined. 'Again, sir, please accept my sympathy! Come, then, and take a seat. Would you like a cup of coffee?'

'Thank you, no. I do not take stimulants of any kind. I find it best, in my profession. With your permission, however, I shall enjoy a cigar while we speak.'

'But of course,' Holmes said, showing him to the cane-backed chair, next to mine. 'Your note mentioned Dr Trevelyan. Have you known him long?'

'Almost a year. He was quite successful in treating a client of mine, who had succumbed to a nervous disorder. He is, I think, a brilliant young physician. Likewise, he has become quite a good friend. He speaks highly of you, Mr Holmes, and how you handled the Blessington affair.'

Holmes bowed slightly. 'It was a singular case,' he replied, as he sank back into his favourite armchair, 'though not terribly difficult. I only wish Blessington had been honest with me from the start. If so, he would likely be alive today.'

Holmes produced Montclair's note from his waistcoat pocket, and eyed it quizzically. 'Now then, Mr Montclair,' he said, 'I wish you to start from scratch. Be as detailed as if you were preparing a legal brief, and tell me of this 'perplexing matter' of which you write.'

Montclair struck a match and lit his La Corona, sending a small cloud of blue smoke swirling to the ceiling. 'It all began on Wednesday last,' he said, 'at our offices on Bond Street. A man was shown in whom I had never met before. His name, he said, was Henri Victoire, and he had come to make a request.

''I am here because your reputation for integrity and discretion are well known,' he said. 'Oh, don't be modest, sir. It most surely is. It is why I wish you to undertake a very delicate mission on my behalf.'

''And that is?'

''I wish you to be my personal courier. To deliver an important letter for me to Bristol.'

''What type of letter? What are the circumstances?'

''Of a private nature, I'm afraid. Oh, there is nothing illegal, I assure you! But it is a business matter, and the letter must be delivered to Mr Warwick, at the Royal Hotel, on Friday.'

''Very well. I'm sure someone from our office can handle the chore.'

''Oh, no, sir!' he insisted. 'Not anyone from your firm; that just won't do! It must be you, sir! I'll trust this matter to no one else.'

'For a moment or two, I hesitated, gentlemen — though not for the reason you think. You see, the *Carpathia* was docking Friday; my late brother's things had been sent home, and naturally, I wished to claim them. But, since Mr Victoire seemed so insistent, I decided to send my man Hayes along instead.

''Very well', I told him, 'I shall deliver your letter to Bristol on Friday. What are your instructions?'

''They are quite simple,' he said. 'Upon arriving in Bristol, take a room at the Royal Hotel. At precisely five o'clock present yourself at the front desk, and inform the concierge you have a letter for Mr Warwick. Once you have seen it placed securely in his box, your duties are fulfilled. You may enjoy dinner at the hotel, and I'm certain you'll be able to catch an early train Saturday morning for your return.'

''And as to expenses?'

''Cost is no matter, Mr Montclair,' he assured me. 'What is paramount is that this letter is delivered to Mr Warwick punctually at five. This, I'm sure, will more than cover your fee and any expenses.'

'At which point, Mr Holmes, he drew two envelopes from his waistcoat pocket. One contained the missive I was to deliver, the other one hundred pounds in notes.'

Holmes whistled. 'A princely sum, indeed!' he exclaimed. 'Especially for what seems so trivial a task. The envelope which contained the letter, what was it like?'

'By its thickness, I'm certain it contained at least two or three sheets of paper. The envelope was blue, sealed with yellow wax. There was no writing upon it, save for Mr Warwick's name, although the crest bore my client's initials, 'H.V.'.'

'I see. Proceed.'

'Everything went off like clockwork. I travelled by train to Bristol, and secured a room at the Royal Hotel. At five o'clock exactly, I turned over the letter, which I then saw placed in Mr Warwick's box. As to dinner, the pheasant and escargots were quite delicious. I returned from Bristol the following morning.'

'But you did not see this Mr Warwick yourself?' Holmes asked.

'No, sir, I did not. Mr Victoire had said that was not necessary; only that I be sure the letter was placed into his box. However, I did enquire Saturday morning, as I was leaving, as to whether the gentleman had indeed claimed his mail. I was told he had, and that he'd checked out some time before. I took that to be the end of it.'

'H'mm,' Holmes mused, 'this is a strange business to be sure. Why pay for the security of a courier, if the letter was not to be placed directly into Warwick's hand? And why such punctuality, when there was no one to meet?'

'My thoughts exactly, sir. And Dr Trevelyan's as well, once he had heard the particulars. We dined on Saturday night at Boodle's; it was then that he urged I consult you.'

For a moment, Holmes said nothing. Behind the half-closed eyes, I knew, his mind was racing.

'And your brother's effects?' I asked. 'They were waiting when you returned?'

'Alas, no, Doctor. Somehow a mistake had been made, and they were not aboard the *Carpathia*. Apologies were given and Hayes was told that Arthur's trunks would most assuredly follow on the *Mauro Elaina*, which docks today.'

'Ah, you are on your way to customs, then?'

'No, worse luck. I've been forced to send poor Hayes again.'

'But why?'

'Because,' our client exclaimed, 'in one hour, I shall be on my way to Bristol again, on behalf of Mr Victoire!'

I could not help but show surprise. Holmes had bolted upright in his chair, suddenly at attention. 'Another letter?' he queried.

'Yes. Exactly like the first. Mr Victoire brought it to my office yesterday, imploring me to represent him one more time. And, he produced another hundred pounds, as well!'

Holmes's eyes were gleaming now; he seemed like a hound who has caught the scent. 'Your instructions — ?'

'They are the same. I am again to leave a letter for Mr Warwick at the Royal Hotel.'

'At five o'clock?'

'At five o'clock.'

A slight smile passed across Holmes's lips. Rising, he walked over to Montclair and reached out his hand. 'Mr Victoire's letter — may I see it?'

Montclair hesitated. 'You may examine it,' he said, finally, drawing a long blue envelope from his coat pocket. 'The contents, you understand, are confidential.'

Holmes's eyes narrowed; it was a look I had seen before.

'You will bear witness, Watson,' he declared, as we walked towards the fireplace, 'that I take full responsibility for my actions!'

In a flash, he plucked his ever-present knife from the mantle, sliced open the envelope, and proceeded to read the pages inside.

'Mr Holmes!' Montclair roared, leaping to his feet. 'This is an outrage, sir! Your rashness will cost me my reputation!'

'If so, you have sold it for very little,' Holmes replied, returning him the papers. 'Any court, I'll wager, would find this a false sale, indeed.'

Montclair and I stood stunned. The pages before us were blank!

'But, but — !' our client stammered. 'What does this mean, sir? What kind of hoax is this?'

'A decidedly expensive one,' I interjected. 'A game someone is willing to spend two hundreds pounds to play.'

Holmes clapped his hands. 'Point well taken, Watson!' he concurred. 'This matter is hardly so shallow. Now, Mr Montclair — if you would — return to your chair and describe this Henri Victoire to me.'

'He is a small, lean fellow — about five feet tall. His hair is black and shiny, and his moustache is twirled and waxed. He is an engaging person, I suppose, though his accent and manner clearly mark him as French. He dresses well, and carries a stick.'

'And does he smoke?'

'Yes, cigarettes. He carries them in a thin, silver case, and uses a holder before smoking.'

Holmes's face appeared grave, though I

could not for the life of me imagine why. 'And your late brother,' he asked, in a softer tone, 'did he have any other interests while he lived in England?'

'Sports, you mean?'

'Yes, or forms of recreation.'

'Well, he followed the cricket matches religiously. Arthur never was much of a player himself, but he'd travel half a day to watch Grace[1] swing. That, and whist, were his two passions.'

'Cards, you say?'

'Yes. Without his Wednesday and Friday nights at the club, I think he might have gone mad this summer, languishing about the Foreign Office. He was quite enthused, when his appointment was finally settled.'

'Ah, he played with you at Boodle's, then?'

'No. He belonged to the Bagatelle; put up last Christmas by a mutual friend. Does it really matter? I — '

Holmes silenced him with a wave of his

---

[1] William Gilbert Grace, premier player of the Victorian era.

hand. 'What matters now, Mr Montclair, is that you put yourself completely in my hands,' he said, severely. 'This is a serious business; far more so than you realise. I have two questions: what time does your train leave for Bristol? And what time is Hayes to meet the boat?'

'I'm to take the eleven o'clock at Paddington,' Montclair answered. 'My luggage is with me, in the cab. The *Mauro Elaina*, I believe, docks at two.'

'Thank God,' Holmes said. 'Had they been reversed, we'd have been hard put. Board your train at eleven, then, and go as far as Reading. When you arrive, get off and catch the first train back, then drive immediately here. Speak to no one, is that clear?'

'Yes, but — '

'Besides Hayes, are there any other servants?'

'Only Emma, the cook.'

'And is there a way the three of us, possibly four, might enter your house undetected?'

Montclair thought a moment. 'The cellar door!' he declared. 'It is located in the rear, and there are evergreens on either side. It is kept locked, but I have a key.'

'Excellent! Then it shall be our passageway later. Watson, fetch Mr Montclair his coat and hat, will you? It is imperative, sir, that you do not miss your train.'

At the door, Montclair protested a final time, but Holmes steadfastly refused to tell him more. 'In good time, you will know all,' my friend assured him, as he buttoned up his wrap. 'But hurry now! And remember, not a word to anyone that you are getting off at Reading; come directly back to Baker Street. On no account, be later than four-thirty! Darkness falls early this time of year.'

As I closed the door on our bewildered friend, I had to admit I was as much in the dark as he. Holmes had obviously detected something quite sinister behind these strange goings-on. But what they had to do with Montclair's home, or the arrival of his dead brother's belongings, I could not fathom.

Silently, I watched as Holmes stoked

the fire, then reached for his favourite clay and the Turkish slipper. When he did not immediately ask for some time alone, I decided to try an opening.

'You have a theory on all this, then?' I asked, taking up my pipe as well.

'It is Moriarty,' Holmes replied, as he struck a match. Outside, the wind whipped angrily at the windows, but it was not that which caused me to shudder slightly.

'And how do you know that?'

'Because the man Montclair described to me was Pierre D'Arcy. I'd bet my life on that.'

'D'Arcy?' I queried, rising to fetch Holmes's directory. 'I do not believe I've heard that name.'

'You'll not find him there, Watson,' my companion said. 'My knowledge of his background, I confess, is still too thin. I do know he was once a tailor and a locksmith, but his deft fingers and mind have found themselves another trade. He has become one of the most successful jewel thieves in Europe, and has recently come into Professor Moriarty's employ.'

'However did you learn that?' I asked.

'Porlock,' Holmes answered, referring to the lone informant he had been able to secure inside Moriarty's gates, at the time of the tragic Birlstone affair.[1] 'My pilot-fish, thank goodness, still chooses to follow the shark, illuminating our way.'

'Was it he who gave you D'Arcy's description?'

'No. I glimpsed his face in the Rogues' Portrait Gallery at the Yard, back in July. In addition to his penchant for snuff, the silver cigarette case and holder were also mentioned.'

'But a jewel thief? I thought that was Colonel Moran's domain?'

'It is an ominous sign, Watson. It suggests that Moriarty is already expanding his operations to the Continent. Moran, no doubt, has been assured primacy inside our shores.'

'You think, then, that some great crime is about to be committed?'

'No, Watson. I know it has already been done.'

---

[1] *The Valley of Fear*, January 7–8, 1888.

'What?'

Holmes went to his desk and rummaged among his clippings, then brought me one from the *Times* which he had not yet pasted into his scrapbook. 'Had you risen at a decent hour this morning, you would have quite likely had knowledge of this,' he said. 'I daresay, it would have given you a whole different perspective on what Montclair was telling us.'

The story, which was headed Rome, Italy, had appeared on September 18, the day after we had departed for Stranraer. It read:

Valuable Jewel Stolen in Italy: Police Baffled

Rome, Italy — Italian authorities reported on Sunday that a widespread search was already under way for thieves who on Saturday night stole the valuable Brereton Emerald from a British diplomat's residence, just outside the city.

The jewel, which belonged to Mrs Abigail Morrison, wife of Sir William

Morrison, the British Ambassador, was taken in the early-morning hours while the house was asleep. The villa, owned by the Duchess Arabella of Cavour, was on loan to the Morrisons for the length of Sir William's stay.

Another resident of the house, Mr Arthur Montclair, was found bound and gagged in the lower hall. Montclair, an aide to Sir William, said he had heard a noise about two in the morning, and upon investigating, was set upon by the thieves.

Montclair, who was rendered unconscious in the struggle, was unable to identify his assailants, but said three or four men had been involved. The Emerald, one of the largest in the world and valued in excess of 10,000 pounds, was apparently rifled from Mrs Morrison's jewelbox, police say, although the lady was never roused.

'Good Lord, Holmes!' I exclaimed. 'Do you really think there is some connection between this robbery and Montclair's trips to Bristol?'

'I do,' he said, puffing his pipe. 'It positively defies the realm of coincidence.'

'But why did Montclair not mention anything of this?'

'Considering the circumstances, I expect he felt it was just another bad memory, Watson. Besides, how could he know it had anything to do with his errands for 'Mr Victoire'? One must also consider the possibility, however scant, that he did not read the *Times* on that given day.'

Holmes strode to the coat rack and pulled down his heavy coat and familiar deerstalker cap.

'You are off, then?' I enquired.

'Yes, I've much to do before Mr Montclair returns. First, I shall rouse someone at the Yard; Lestrade or Gregson, whichever I can find. After which, I shall surreptitiously investigate Montclair's residence in Brixton. Since we will be venturing out in darkness, I must be sure of the lay of the land. Once matters unfold, we will have no second chance.'

'Shall I accompany you?'

'It is not necessary; in fact, I shall be better off alone, in the matter of Montclair's house.'

'I see. Brixton? That is a jaunt.'

'Yes. Luckily, the Yard is on my way. Barring the unforeseen, I shall return around four.' Holmes paused at the door. 'And Watson,' he added, 'do be good enough to clean and load your army revolver while I'm gone. D'Arcy is not a man to be taken lightly.'

Although I tried to keep myself busy, the afternoon seemed to drag on for an eternity. First, remembering Holmes's instructions, I brought out my Webley and cleaned it thoroughly, also taking care to insert fresh ammunition. That done, I perused the latest editions of the *Chronicle* and *Telegraph*, brought up by Mrs Hudson. After which, I poured myself a glass of Pattison's over ice, laid my feet close to the fire, and delved into Boothby's *A Brighton Tragedy* for the better part of two hours. It was slow-going, though through no fault of the author; my mind, I found, simply could not resist dwelling upon the unusual aspects of Howard Montclair's story, and how it might somehow be linked to the infamous jewel robbery in Rome.

About three-thirty, I heard the front bell, and Mrs Hudson again brought up our client. After pouring him a brandy, I rang for cucumber sandwiches and tea (knowing from previous experience, that once we found ourselves upon the trail, dinner might well be little and late). Holmes arrived back promptly at four, stamping his feet to shake off the dampness as he hung his coat and hat upon the rack.

'Gregson has not arrived as yet, I see,' my friend remarked, as he rubbed his hands together before the fire. 'Ah, there's the bell! That will be him, I'm sure. Ah, Gregson! Welcome! You have made our party complete.'

The tall, flaxen-haired inspector — who only weeks before had worked with us in the unfortunate Kratides affair[1] — shook

---

[1] *The Case of the Greek Interpreter*, September 12, 1888.

Holmes's hand. 'I've come as you requested, Mr Holmes,' he said. 'It is the least that I can do, considering your past favours. Why it seems like only yesterday that you helped us with that Drebber business.[1] And this, I take it, is Mr Montclair?'

'Yes. It is to his house in Brixton that we'll soon be travelling. You have, I hope, carried out my instructions?'

'To the letter. The bullseye lamps are in the carriage, and I've brought four strong constables, as well.' Gregson patted the pocket of his coat. 'Like myself, they are well armed.'

'A worthy precaution, I assure you. We play a dangerous game tonight, Gregson. The stakes are high. But if we are successful, your catch will be extraordinary.'

'Who is this catch, then, that we require such a heavy net?'

'Pierre D'Arcy.'

The policeman's jaw sagged. 'D'Arcy! The Frenchman? Heaven help us, we are

---

[1] *A Study in Scarlet*, March 4–7, 1881.

stepping up in company! I wasn't aware the scoundrel was in the country.'

'If all goes well,' Holmes told him, 'he shall be in your hands quite soon. I only ask one favour, Gregson: let me direct the game. Time is short, and we must be off. Agreed?'

Gregson squirmed a bit. The situation was clearly not to his liking. Yet what else could he do, save trust Sherlock Holmes once more? 'Agreed,' he said.

An hour later, we were in Brixton. Howard Montclair's residence was one of a row of elegant houses not far from King's College Hospital, near the woods off Cold Harbour Lane. Upon Holmes's instruction, we alighted from our cab some distance away, and quickly walked round to the rear of the property in the growing darkness, while Gregson's men positioned themselves in the shadows, behind a garden wall across the way.

As we crouched next to a hedge, I could just make out the edge of the cellar door to which Montclair had referred, lying between thick bushes that buttressed tall windows on either side. All was dark, save for a light that shone from the right front corner of the structure, which faced out towards the street.

'But that's the sitting room!' Montclair exclaimed. 'What could Hayes or Emma be doing there? Their quarters are in the rear.'

'You will note it is not the entire room that's lit, but only a single lamp,' Holmes observed. 'It is a signal, clearly.'

'Signal — ?'

'Montclair, I must be frank. It is my strong belief that your servants have betrayed you.'

'Mr Holmes — !'

'Quiet! From now on, we speak in whispers, and only when it is necessary! Montclair, you go first, and unlock and raise the cellar door. Quietly, remember! Then signal us, and we shall join you in the shadows, one by one.'

Bending low, the solicitor crossed the lawn, disappearing into the darkness beneath the shrubs. As we waited, I could not help but shiver; it was not a pleasant night to be about. Beneath me, the ground was cold and damp, and the wind's raw bite stung against my face. Finally, we saw the waving motion of Montclair's arm: First Holmes, then Gregson, and last myself, sprinted across the grass.

'Down the stair, and quick!' Holmes hissed, as we crouched before the pitch black opening. 'Gregson, you go first! Once in, light your lantern. Watson, you will lower the cellar door behind you, after we have passed.'

When I saw the gleam from Gregson's lamp, I immediately did as Holmes had asked, easing the heavy door shut above me as I backed slowly down the concrete steps. To my dismay, the door's iron hinges creaked mightily; I could only hope the harsh rustling of the wind among the bushes would drown out any noise.

'Thank you, Watson,' Holmes whispered, as he struck a match to light his lamp. 'Should a scout come round, nothing will seem amiss. Now . . . '

Slowly, my companion swung his lantern back and forth, about the darkened cellar before us — revealing a cluttered array of boxes and crates, buckets and tools, an old cupboard which held stacks of papers, and even shelves of jarred preserves — until its beam finally rested upon another stairway some distance away.

'Where does it lead?' he asked Montclair, his voice so low I could barely hear.

'Into a small cloakroom, at the end of the hall,' the other whispered back. 'The entrance is covered by a curtain.'

'Is there room for all of us?'

'Yes.'

'Good. From there we shall keep our vigil. Now, look sharp all of you, as we make our way! A clatter of any kind will certainly rouse the house.'

For me, the next few minutes seemed an eternity, as we carefully stepped our way across the damp and musty cellar, following as best we could the twin beams of Holmes's and Gregson's lamps before us. As we passed the shelves of fruits and vegetables, I suddenly gasped, as my shoulder brushed against something and sent it flying! To my great relief, Holmes's light showed it to be nothing more than a bag of onions stored in for the winter, swinging harmlessly from a rafter.

We climbed the stairs without incident, and passed through a door into a room not five feet square. Holmes and Gregson quickly extinguished their lights, as the cloakroom was partially illuminated from the light of the hallway outside. Trying to be as quiet as possible, we huddled together in that small, close cubicle, with coats and boots all round us, and a shelf of hats and scarves above our heads — all made vaguely visible by an inch-wide band of light which separated the bottom of the curtain from the floor.

Holmes opened the curtain slightly with his index finger. Standing behind him the rest of us could see nothing; but the voices of a man and woman engaged in heated conversation could be clearly heard.

' — should have been here by now, John Hayes! They knew the *Mauro Elaina* made port at two.'

'Here, now! The man said the pickup wouldn't be made 'til dark — and then only if they saw the light! Why, it's only been a quarter hour since you set it on the ledge.'

'All the same, I wish his baggage had just arrived on Friday! We'd be done with it by now!'

'An incidental, woman! An incidental! The trunks are here, aren't they? What difference is a day or two? You've got your sovereigns, same as me!'

'That's easy for you to say! What if Mr Montclair returns tonight?'

'He won't! Don't you understand? They've planned this smart; he's gone away to Bristol again.'

'And what after that? If he ever finds out, we've sold our reputations, sure! Oh, I wish I'd never got involved in any o' this!'

'Emma Simpson, either cork it or take a slug to calm your nerves! The man told me: what he wants from these here trunks won't arouse anyone's suspicion.'

'Hah! That's easy for him to say: his neck's not on the — '

At that moment, two sharp rings of the doorbell interrupted the woman's lament.

Edging myself a bit further to Holmes's

right, I was able at last to peer out through the thin slit he had drawn before him in the curtain. In the hallway, I saw a woman I took to be Emma Simpson, the nervous cook, wringing her hands fervently in the folds of her long apron. On the floor beside her sat two large black steamer trunks, which had undoubtedly borne home the belongings of the late Arthur Montclair. John Hayes was nowhere to be seen, having obviously gone to the door.

'Ready now!' Holmes whispered to us. 'Remember, Gregson, I shall make the move! Timing is essential, for we must catch them in the very act!'

I have never been a squeamish man; but at that instant, my mouth grew dry. Resolutely, I drew my pistol from my coat.

Other voices were in the hall. As Holmes again peered out, I caught sight of a small, well-dressed man with a black moustache, who I knew must be D'Arcy. With him was Hayes, followed by a surly-looking rough in a badly-worn overcoat and bowler hat. If there was trouble, I felt instinctively, he would be the man.

'Ah, you have done well, Hayes!' the small fellow declared, as he rushed over to the trunks. Crouching down, he ran his hand across their smooth dark finish. 'Oh yes, you surely have.'

Noticing the cook's apprehension, he flashed her his warmest smile. 'You appear upset, dear lady,' he said, solicitously. 'Oh, do not be. Do not! This is a simple errand; in a few moments, I shall be gone, and none will be the wiser.'

Turning back to Hayes, the smile froze upon his face. 'You have not tried to open them, I hope?'

'Not on my life, sir,' Hayes assured him. 'There's nothing in a dead man's goods for me.'

'A wise — and appropriate — sentiment. You have the keys?'

Hayes handed them over.

Quickly, the little man opened the trunk nearest him and began to rifle through it. Deftly, his hands searched among the stacks of neatly-packed suits and shirts, shoes and socks, ties and toilet articles — always careful, when the work was done, to rearrange perfectly, so as nothing appeared disturbed.

It was as he started to burrow through the second trunk that we heard his cry of triumph.

Before him, D'Arcy held what appeared to be a small glass jar of cleansing cream. With a look of satisfaction, he carefully unscrewed the lid, and then, using his two front fingers, he dug into the pearl-white lotion and scooped out a fair-sized blob. Putting down the jar, he drew a kerchief from his pocket, and began to wipe furiously at the mess.

Before my eyes, the white suddenly turned to green! The clearest, deepest shade of green I had ever seen, reflecting sparks of light this way and that.

My mouth dropped. What he held in his hand, I realised, was nothing less than the missing Brereton Emerald!

'I shall take that now, D'Arcy!' Holmes commanded, as he stepped from behind the curtain. 'Or should I say, 'Henri Victoire'?'

Uttering an oath in his native tongue,

the Frenchman swung round in amazement, as we all advanced upon him — Holmes with his hand outstretched, Gregson and I with pistols drawn. As we closed, the little man's eyes narrowed menacingly.

Suddenly, from the corner of my eye, I saw the rough go for his coat! Heeding Holmes's advice, I fired without hesitation. For a heartbeat, the hall was filled by the sound of the shot, and Emma Simpson's terrified scream; as the big man grasped his arm, a revolver clattered to the floor.

D'Arcy, too, in that split second, had sought a weapon. But Holmes's quick kick had caught his shoulder — sending his dagger flying.

'All right, now!' Gregson roared. 'That will be enough of that! You are all under arrest!'

Montclair, standing a step behind Gregson, seemed as shocked as if someone had pole-axed him. Hayes, unable to meet his master's angry stare, glanced down at the floor; Simpson began to weep.

'Hurry, Gregson!' Holmes implored. 'Call your men! There surely is a cab outside!'

Before the policeman could step out front, we heard shouting in the street. A second later, a shot was fired, and then another. After that, all was silent.

As Gregson threw open the door, a uniformed constable rushed inside, pistol in hand.

'We got 'em all, sir!' he declared. 'The driver of the coach tried to pull a gun — I settled with him myself! I know our orders were to wait for the whistle, but we were afraid they might be off. We took things on our own, when we heard the shot inside.'

Gregson clapped him on the shoulder. 'No apologies necessary, Sergeant!' he told the man. 'You and your men acted well. You've all earned your pay and a pint, this night!'

D'Arcy snarled, as Holmes reached down and gently plucked the valuable jewel from his hand.

'I must commend you,' my friend remarked, as he held the gleaming gem up to the light. 'Your choice of a hiding place was brilliant! Had you not shown it to us yourself, I doubt anyone would have guessed.'

'And who are you?' the Frenchman enquired, with a testy sneer. 'I'm certain no ordinary policeman handled this.'

Holmes waved Gregson to silence before he could protest. 'I am Sherlock Holmes, a private investigator,' he declared, 'acting on behalf of Mr Howard Montclair — whose brother you have murdered!'

D'Arcy glared. Seldom have I seen such hate in a person's eyes. 'You are too clever for your own good, I think,' he replied, his voice dripping with malevolence. 'You — !' D'Arcy suddenly drew silent and composed himself; a thin, cruel smile crossed his face. 'Prove it, then,' he added. 'I have nothing more to say.'

Holmes masked his disappointment with a smile of his own. The Frenchman had refused to take his bait. 'Ah, well, then, Gregson!' he cried. 'They are yours to carry off. I'm sure there are some vacant cots down at the Yard. Here! The honour of returning the stone is also yours! Did I not promise an extraordinary catch?'

The flaxen-haired inspector beamed. 'You did, indeed!' he stated, as D'Arcy and the others were being cuffed and led away. 'However, there are a few things I wish you would explain. How did you come to know of this — that the Brereton Emerald was being brought into the country?'

Briefly, Holmes related to Gregson the events which had occurred that very morning: Howard Montclair's strange story of his employment as a courier by the mysterious 'Henri Victoire', the later revelation of the fake letter, and his earlier discovery from clipping the papers that the young Montclair had been in the Morrison villa at the time the jewel was taken.

'My attention was aroused the moment Mr Montclair told us of his brother's position in Rome,' Holmes explained. 'Of course, I had read the story, Watson; you had not. The offer to travel to Bristol was bizarre, indeed. How much more so, then, when Montclair was contacted a second time — and again on the very day his brother's effects were due to arrive? The conclusion was obvious: Someone wanted him out of the city, in order to gain access to the brother's luggage. But why?

'The answer became crystal clear, once Montclair had described 'Henri Victoire' to me. Pierre D'Arcy had stolen the emerald, and was smuggling it into England! Quite likely, a buyer had already been arranged. Since Hayes was responsible for securing the trunks, I was reasonably certain he was involved.'

'Poor Arthur,' Montclair lamented. 'Why on earth would they murder him? They had the jewel, and were away.'

Holmes tossed me a warning glance as he began to speak. 'According to the newspaper account,' he replied, 'your brother surprised the thieves that night. I imagine they feared he might somehow identify them later. Now, Gregson! Is there anything more you wish to know?'

'Not a thing, Mr Holmes. You have explained it all quite satisfactorily. I have D'Arcy, and the emerald. You mark my words, gentlemen! He'll do time, once the evidence is brought to the Assizes. Though, without a body, I doubt a murder charge can stick.'

Holmes nodded in agreement. 'Alas,' he said, 'I fear you are correct. Well, then! Good evening to you, Mr Montclair! And what a remarkable evening it has been! We have not only provided the solution to your eccentric little problem, but served the public good as well. You will give our regards to Dr Trevelyan, I hope, the very next time you meet?'

Once in the cab, I could restrain myself no longer. Holmes, I knew, was holding something back — and I was determined to learn exactly of its nature.

'I caught that look you gave me, Holmes,' I ventured. 'Why do you really think young Arthur Montclair was killed?'

'There we move into the realms of conjecture, Watson,' he answered. 'Simply because of the logistics involved, my reasons must be based more upon that than fact.'

'Well, by all means, tell me then.'

'You recall what Montclair said about

his brother's languishing about the Foreign Office all summer?'

'Yes. Following the cricket matches and playing whist — ' Suddenly it hit me. ' — at the Bagatelle Club!'

'Exactly! The haunt of Colonel Sebastian Moran.'

'Good Lord! I gather what you're driving at! If Moran played foul — as he has been rumoured to do — then it is conceivable the young Montclair might have found himself considerably in his debt.'

' — A debt which was called in, most likely by D'Arcy, once Montclair had established himself in Rome.'

'Ah, you think he was involved, then?'

'I do, Watson. Every sense, every intuition that I possess tells me it was so. You recall what the newspaper account described concerning Mrs Morrison?'

'No, I'm afraid that I do not.'

'It reported that the emerald had been taken from her personal jewelbox, presumably in her bedroom. And yet, she was not awakened. That immediately suggests two things: first, that the thieves knew exactly where to look — '

'Information which had been supplied!'

' — And, that the lady's slumber had most likely been induced by more than the events of a busy day! She was given a sleeping draught, I'll wager, by someone who knew her habits well.'

'The young Montclair, you mean!'

Holmes shrugged. 'He certainly had the opportunity, Watson. As well as being able to allow D'Arcy and his confederates silent access during the night — after which, it was made to appear that a struggle had taken place.'

'That's all well and good. But if Montclair was in it with them, why on earth did they murder him? They had the jewel; and if Montclair later went to the authorities, his own reputation was forfeit.'

'True, but it was a chance they could not take. Arthur Montclair was the only man alive who could link D'Arcy and the emerald to Moran. Do you think for a moment that Moriarty would risk leaving both his chief lieutenants unguarded? A change of heart by Montclair, and who knows? The professor may have even found himself standing in the dock.'

'The blackguards! They took him forcibly up the mountain, then?'

'I cannot prove it. But I sincerely doubt a man who is so unwieldy at cricket would decide to risk life and limb upon the slopes. Sport was not his cup of tea.'

I was overcome by a sense of deep frustration — and horror. Through my mind flashed a picture of the young Montclair, drugged and helpless, being thrown from some high cliff . . .

'But is there nothing we can do?' I demanded. 'Surely, if we told all this to the police — !'

'To what end, Watson? Moriarty's alibis are secure; you may count on that. Moran? Our only link to him is gone. Ah, well. At least we have D'Arcy. Moriarty's move to the Continent has been delayed. Lord help us, should his net ever spread that far! Given his genius, and powers of organisation, the possibilities for high intrigue are immense.'

'If only Moriarty had been waiting in that cab outside tonight,' I speculated.

'What a boon to mankind that would have been!'

'Hah!' Holmes laughed. 'He is too clever for that, Watson! Big Ben will chime thirteen, before Moriarty is caught lurking near. D'Arcy I expected; the game was too big to trust another. But the professor? — no, no. Had you asked, I would have cheerfully wagered every shilling I owned that we'd not see him this night.'

In spite of my sombre mood, I could not help but smile just a little. How could I have imagined that — for one of the few times in his career — events were about to prove Holmes wrong?

Some time later, our cab rattled to a halt before our familiar rooms at Baker Street. As we alighted, I noticed the avenue was deserted — save for a shabbily-dressed fellow who stood before our very door, fidgeting noticeably as he rubbed his ungloved hands together in an attempt to combat the cold.

As my eyes met his, I felt a vague uneasiness; there was clearly recognition in his look. Returning his gaze with steel,

I placed my hand again about my revolver, which had served us so well not long before.

'Beggin' yer pardon, sirs,' he said, stepping forward as Holmes and I approached. 'A gentleman desires to speak with Mr Holmes — in the cab.'

His nod indicated an elegant-looking four-wheeler, which sat beneath the street lamp across the way.

Holmes and I exchanged a glance.

'It shall be both or none,' I told him. 'I shall not allow it otherwise.'

'There is no danger,' the other said. 'I was bound to tell you that.'

In spite of his assurances, a coldness crept up the small of my back; my uneasiness would not go away. I was determined not to be deterred.

'Holmes, I must insist — !'

My friend silenced me by raising his hand . . . And, as I was sure I detected, a faint smile of appreciation. 'You have heard the terms,' he told the man, coldly. 'I suggest you convey them to your master.'

The fellow fairly sprinted across the

cobblestones. For a moment, as he stood beside the cab, we heard the murmur of voices. Then he turned, and waved us forward.

I kept my grip upon my pistol, as we climbed into that carriage. A sense of overriding danger pervaded the chilly night air. Across from us, a lone passenger was seated, almost engulfed within the shadow. And yet, from the glow of the nearby street light, I could just make out those cold, forbidding features, which at a later date, I would first reveal to my many readers[1] — the tall, thin form with rounded shoulders, the receding grey hair above a large forehead that domed out in a curve. And, perhaps most frightening, the lifeless, menacing, coal-black shark eyes, puckered and blinking, which were deeply sunken into the recesses of his pale, almost skeleton-like head.

I started. Before me, I realised was Moriarty himself. The scholar and master schemer . . . and, as Holmes had

[1] *The Final Problem*, April 24–May 4, 1891.

oft-times reminded me, the most dangerous man in London. For an instant, my
mind began to race like a runaway train.
Should I pull my pistol now, no matter
the cost, and rid England — nay, the
world — of this diabolical madman?

'I would advise you to release the
revolver, Doctor,' he said to me, as if he
had read my very thoughts. 'You really
must, you know! Another movement of
your right hand, and I shall be compelled
to pull the trigger myself — which will
mean nothing to you, sir, but the end to
your illustrious companion.' The ogre
smiled. 'Dear me, it would be such a
waste,' he added, 'since, I assure you, I
have no such independent thought in
mind.'

I shrank from the demon's omnipo-
tence. Was he bluffing? I could not take
the chance. My life, in exchange for his, I
felt, was little enough. But that of Holmes
was far too great a price to pay.

Purposely exaggerating the motion, I
withdrew my hand from the pocket of my
coat, and rested it upon my leg.

'Tell us what you wish, then — Mr

Moriarty!' Holmes said. 'It is a bitter night, and I am not accustomed to doing business in the street.'

'My apologies, sir,' he replied, in his soft, precise fashion, 'but given the events of the evening, it was absolutely necessary.' The cruel smile returned. 'You see, I am at this moment attending *Macbeth* at the Lyceum, with several friends.' Checking his watch, he added, 'Five past eight. The curtain has just risen.'

'Some friends, perhaps,' Holmes retorted, 'but not Pierre D'Arcy.'

The smile froze. 'That is why I am here. You have caused me a great inconvenience, sir; a buyer had been secured.'

'I suspected as much.'

'What I wish to know is: why? You seem an intelligent fellow. Dear me, I have been impressed by some of your recent exploits. You even uncovered my little scheme in Durham — '

'High praise, indeed!'

' — Yet, it is a pity, in recent months, that our paths have begun to cross so frequently. Tonight, I believe, is the fifth occasion since March.'

'I fully anticipate, barring your return to academia, that they shall continue to cross even more,' Holmes told him, evenly. 'My life is devoted to combating crime, and you are the master criminal who plagues this city.'

'High praise, returned!' Moriarty declared, mincing out the words. His manner, I noted had become more agitated; his head had begun to oscillate slightly, from side to side. 'That must not happen, sir! Really, it must not! Until tonight, you have been only an infrequent nuisance; now, I must consider you a positive threat. Should you continue this course — '

'Our conversation is over, Mr Moriarty!' Holmes interrupted. 'To continue it can serve no purpose. Come, Watson — it has been a rewarding night, all told! I am ravenous for some dinner!'

As we stepped down into the street, Moriarty called out Holmes's name once more. 'I am a patient man, sir,' he said, a cold hatred in his dark eyes. 'Please, think over what I have said. Please, do! I hope, most fervently, that I shall not have to speak with you again!'

'When . . . you do,' Holmes replied, trembling with emotion, 'I trust you will have the courtesy to call upon me at my residence, during normal hours. This has been most inconvenient.'

Moriarty snarled, as he closed the carriage door. His driver immediately applied the whip, and the coach clattered off at a furious pace.

'Good Lord, Holmes!' I exclaimed, as I watched the cab disappear into the night. 'I feel as though I've just met Satan himself.'

'Perhaps you have, Watson,' Holmes rejoined. 'Perhaps you have. Unfortunately, I fear, we shall see much more of his evil handiwork in days to come.'

Holmes clapped a hand upon my shoulder; a faint smile crossed his face. 'For now, however, I recommend a glass of claret, and some repast from Mrs Hudson's larder; this round belongs to us.'

Moriarty's Fiendish Plan

Upon reflection, one is apt to note that there are certain dates and occasions during a person's life upon this planet which he or she never forgets; things like birthdays, anniversaries, holidays (the Queen's Jubilee, of course), or perhaps, tragically, the event of a loved one's passing.

For me, November 17, 1888, was just such a day. Even now, more than thirty years later, I cannot recall what transpired on that horrible Saturday without still feeling a shudder of both revulsion and shame — and too, a sense of immense relief as well, considering what nearly occurred. As Sherlock Holmes's biographer, I must record it as the day upon which he and the insidious Professor Moriarty crossed paths for yet a third time so late in that busy year. As Holmes's friend, I must admit that, save for my wounding during the awful slaughter at Maiwand, no other event in my lifetime has been — or remained — so painful and shocking.

It was an especially grey and wintry day. Snow had fallen the night before, leaving London covered in a blanket of white, with frost upon the window panes and icicles hanging from the trees. The skies were cloudy and rough, promising more snow; the streets a muddy brown, where the wheels of cabs and carts, and the wagons of sundry vendors, had tracked and trampled this latest layer of the fluffy stuff into a wet and slippery slush.

The cold, damp weather, I knew full well, would do my old leg wound no good. None the less, I was determined to undertake an afternoon walk that day — and not merely because (as Holmes would most surely insist) it had become a habit of late. In addition to fresh air and exercise, I also sought a box of La Coronas from the tobacconist, and a shave and a haircut at the barbers as well. Reason enough, I felt, to trek out-of-doors on such a sloppy day. Thus, at a few minutes past one — after lunching on Mrs Hudson's delicious steak and kidney pie, braced by slices of hardy Stilton cheese — I pulled on my togs and took to the streets, leaving Holmes curled up before the fire in his favourite armchair, perusing the morning dailies.

Not a day has passed since I left him thus, that I have not sorely regretted that journey.

As Holmes would tell me later, it was not a half-hour after I had gone that our old friend, Inspector Lestrade of Scotland Yard, had come knocking at our door, seeking my companion's counsel once again.

'I do apologise for bothering you on a Saturday, Mr Holmes,' the lean police-man said, as he stepped inside. 'In fact, I should not have bothered you at all, save I know your taste for that which is uncommon, no matter how trivial it might at first appear.'

Holmes closed the door behind him and rubbed his palms together gleefully, anticipating a fresh problem was at hand.

'My dear Lestrade! It is no bother at

all,' he insisted, motioning his visitor to a chair. 'You know I am always obliged, when you see fit to call and apprise me of new developments. Sit down, and warm yourself. The cigars are in the scuttle. Would you care for some coffee, or tea?'

'Thank you, no,' the other said, 'although I shall enjoy a cigar.'

'Ah, these 'Crimson Vandals' have you nettled, then?'

Lestrade shot Holmes an irritated glance. He had, after all, hardly had time to remove his coat and hat. 'And what makes you think that?' he asked, a bit defensively, as he sank into my comfortable chair, beside the bearskin rug.

Holmes regarded him with some amusement. 'Why, the very fact that you are here!' he exclaimed, reaching for his pipe and the Persian slipper. 'Come, come, Lestrade — what else could it be? The papers are full of little else; they state you are in charge of the case. And yet, to date, not one arrest! What is it now? Three incidents in seven days? Or rather, I imagine four — as you have obviously just come from a meadow in Kensington, to finally seek my advice.'

Lestrade sat back, nearly dropping the cigar he had just drawn. Had Holmes leaned down and struck his brow with the stem of his charred black clay, I doubt if he would have shown more surprise. 'But, but — who told you?' he spluttered. 'How on earth — '

Holmes silenced his protestations with a knowing look and a wave of his hand. 'My dear Inspector! It is no mystery. The stub in your waistcoat pocket tells me you rode the Underground this morning. Your cheeks are flushed, your shoes are soggy, and your cuffs are damp — for nigh upon two inches!'

'That could have happened in the street,' Lestrade retorted. 'It snowed last night; they are a mess.'

'Only if the street were paved with clay,' Holmes observed. He took a second to light his pipe, then directed his full attention to the policeman's dampened shoes. 'You must admit, Lestrade, the reddish hue is really quite distinctive. Kensington, without a doubt! And what of those blades of grass, crushed between your soles! Is it too much to suppose, then, that a fourth act has been discovered? This time in a field or pasture, where the green of nature grows so free?'

Lestrade sighed, a defeated look upon his ferret-like face. 'You are correct, Mr Holmes,' he admitted. 'The latest desecration took place in a cemetery, behind Brompton Oratory, just south of Trinity Church. Twelve headstones were knocked flat, all told, and some hammered into pieces. As before, red paint was smeared about everywhere, upon the broken stones, and some that were not touched.'

'And there was another message?'

The policeman stiffened. 'Yes, if you wish to call it that.'

'And what would you call it, Lestrade?'

'Crazy scribbling, more like. A ruse, a joke. A vagrant's dialect.' Lestrade stuck a match and lit his cigar, producing thin blue clouds that arched quickly towards the ceiling. 'This is a queer business, Mr Holmes,' he added. 'A queer business, I must say. I admit we've not one clue so far, but Lord knows, it's not for trying.

166

The word's gone out, a price been set; yet our informants can tell us nothing.'

'And so you've come to me?'

'Yes. I — that is to say, the Yard — would appreciate any direction you can supply. Royal Albert Hall, St Paul's Cathedral, St James's and now the Oratory — this defacement of our national monuments cannot go on. You've read last night's *Evening Standard*, I presume? Already the cry is up in Parliament. Anarchy, Mr Holmes! That is what they fear.'

For a few moments, Holmes sat silently, puffing upon his tried black clay. Then he sprawled back across his armchair, and crossed his legs and closed his eyes, almost as if asleep. 'You are correct, Lestrade,' he murmured. 'Anarchy will not do. Lay out the facts before me, then. Tell all, and I shall endeavour to be of what help I can.'

Lestrade drew out his notebook. 'Actually, I have very little else to report, apart from what has appeared in the papers,' he began. 'Let me see — the vandals struck first on Saturday, the tenth, attacking the Prince Albert Statue off Consort Road. The head of the statue, as well as those of the seated figures below, had all been painted red, and the inscription was splattered as well. A short row of lettering was also found, neatly inscribed across the marble base. Sergeant Mayhew brought it to my attention, as soon as I arrived.'

'And what time was this?'

'About eight in the morning. The damage had been discovered by a constable on his round, and I was sent for immediately.'

'There was no mention of this lettering in the papers.'

'No. I copied it down, then had it scrubbed off, before anyone else arrived. No sense in revealing all our cards, I felt, until we were ready to play our hand.'

'In that case,' Holmes said, 'I hope you were precise. Proceed.'

'Their next target,' Lestrade continued, 'was the statue of Queen Anne, in front of the cathedral, upon the night of the thirteenth. She was painted red, just like the Prince, and there was a second row of lettering. This time, I was not quick enough, however, which is why you read of it in the papers. After that, we would hardly deny that such messages existed — though, naturally, we refused to make them public.'

The policeman flicked his ash into the fire. 'Lord help the officer who let that slip,' he remarked with exasperation. 'If I ever learn his name, he'll sign in next on Queer Street! Now, where was I? Oh, yes. Incident number three occurred on Thursday last, in St James's Square — '

'Let me guess,' Holmes interrupted. 'William III, this time?'

'Exactly. Little wonder, then, that certain people — rather distinguished people, if you catch my meaning — are quite upset. Three monarchs painted the colour of blood, and now this business in a graveyard! You don't have to look far, Mr Holmes, to draw an inference from that.'

'Hardly. You have questioned the known subversives, I take it? Abrams, Clark and their like?'

'We have. But, so far, all trails have run

cold. Yet, if not them, it's someone close. Why, the motive's plain as day!'

'You have examined each site closely? There were no footprints, or marks about?'

'Not a one, Mr Holmes. We are of a mind there; that was what I searched for first. I mean, tossing all that paint about in the dark, you know. You assume someone must have stepped in something. But, no such luck! For vandals, they were a tidy bunch.'

'Well, then, the most important point: these messages, Lestrade — what do they say?'

'I wish that I could tell you, Mr Holmes. The truth is, I cannot read them!'

Holmes sat bolt upright in his chair. This time, it was his turn to be surprised. 'You cannot read them?'

'No. As I said before, they're scribbling gibberish. Even Gregson, though he hated to admit it, couldn't make head nor tail of them. Still, knowing your bent for things such as this, I brought them along, just the same.'

Lestrade handed Holmes a single sheet of paper, upon which the following four lines were written:

ᛗᛁᚱᚱᛁᚱ ᛗᚯᛏ ᛋᛁᚠᛗᚱᚿᚱᚱ ᚻᛗᚱ

ᚻᚯᚠᛏ ᛗᚯᛏ ᚱᚠᛗᚱᚿᚱᚱ ᛋᛗᛗᚱᛏ ᛋᚠ

ᛗᚷᚻᛗᛐᚠᚱᛐ ᚱᛐᚠ ᛋᛁᚠᛗᚱᚿᚱᚱ ᚻᛗᚱ

ᛋᚷᚿᚠᛏᛋ ᚿᛏᚒᚱᛏ ᚱᛐᛗᚱ ᚿᚱᛁᚿᚹ ᚻᚿᛁᛏᛗᛒ

In a flash, Holmes was on his feet and at his desk, magnifying glass in hand. For some long moments, he studied the figures intently, while Lestrade frowned and fidgeted behind him.

'Well, Mr Holmes, what have we here?' he asked, when at length my friend finally put down his glass. 'Some sort of secret code, I imagine?'

Holmes chuckled. 'My dear Inspector, your choice of words is remarkably apropos!' he stated. 'More so, I'll wager, than you fully understand. You see, this is not merely 'a' secret code — it is one of the oldest secret codes in history! What we have before us are messages written in runes.'

'Runes? And whatever are they?'

'Characters of the earliest written alphabet,' Holmes explained, as he re-lit his pipe, 'used even before the time of Christ. The word 'rune', itself, Lestrade, means 'secret' or 'to whisper'; heathen priests used them for their charms and magic spells. A fitting choice, you must admit, in which to conceal a missive.'

The lean policeman thought that over a moment, a frown upon his face. 'Agreed. But why go to all the trouble, Mr Holmes? What good is it, I ask you, to leave messages no one else can read?'

'A valid point. And yet, mark my words, there is a purpose to it, or it would not have been so deliberately — or carefully — done. Forget your gang of anarchistic roughs, Lestrade. There is a deeper purpose to this.'

'That is all well and good for you to say, Mr Sherlock Holmes,' the other replied, 'but I must report to Whitehall this very afternoon. What am I to tell those gentlemen you propose to do?'

'You may assure them I am giving the case my fullest attention, Lestrade. And that it is my belief, based on what we know, that the crown is not in danger. As to these messages — might I retain them for a day? A visit to the British Museum, I'm sure, will tell us much. They are copied down, I take it, in the order in which the incidents occurred?'

'They are. The last, as you can see, I pencilled in this morning.'

'Excellent! Hallo, is that the front bell? Watson, no doubt, returning from his appointed rounds. Yes, that is his footstep upon the stair. Now then, Lestrade! Keep sharp, and should these Crimson Vandals strike again, touch nothing, and send for me immediately — '

It was at that point, Holmes informed me later, that I opened the door and entered the room — looking, he said, somewhat dazed and confused. What he and Lestrade did not know, of course, was that I had one purpose in mind, as I

173

walked across the room to greet them.

'Ah, Watson!' Holmes exclaimed. 'Back — ?'

Without hesitation, I drew a revolver from my coat, aimed it squarely at Holmes, and fired.

★ ★ ★

I shall always be thankful for Holmes's ability to react so quickly, and Lestrade's bulldog tenacity. These qualities were, at that awful moment, what saved the day, Holmes waiting until the very last instant, as he watched my finger tighten upon the trigger, then leaping aside almost simultaneously with the shot. And Lestrade, at that same second, lunging forward and knocking me to the floor, causing my aim to go far wide.

It was the explosion of the gunshot that awoke me; I opened my eyes feeling groggy and somewhat weak. My mind was blank, my senses numb. The acrid smell of gunpowder was in the air. As my blurred vision began to clear, I could make out Holmes above me, looking apprehensive and concerned, as Lestrade quickly wrested the pistol from my hand. It was only then I began to realise that some sort of terrible mishap had just occurred — a tragedy in which I was somehow involved!

'Holmes!' I cried out, my thoughts a panic. 'What is the matter? My God, what is going on?'

Before either man could answer, our door burst open, and a uniformed constable rushed in. 'And what's this all about, now?' he demanded. 'You there, put down that gun!'

Lestrade bristled, as only he could do. 'I'll give the orders here, constable!' he retorted angrily, rising to his feet. 'I am Inspector Lestrade of Scotland Yard, and this is Mr Sherlock Holmes! As you can plainly see, an accident has taken place, but we have things well in hand!'

The fellow paled visibly before Lestrade's indignation. 'Yes, sir,' he said, taking two steps back. 'Just doing my duty, sir. I was walking past, when I heard a shot. Er, would you like me to fetch a doctor, sir?'

'I doubt if that will be necessary,'

Holmes informed him. 'A moment, however, until we get Watson to his chair.'

As he and Lestrade lowered me into my familiar seat, Holmes noted my left shirt cuff, which was hanging loose, and quickly pulled back my sleeve. Two inches below the elbow joint, a tiny red needle mark could be seen.

'It is as I suspected,' Holmes commented. 'He has been drugged.'

'The scoundrels! Can you remember anything, Doctor?'

'Only the dank smell of the river, Lestrade,' I answered, wearily, my poor head still throbbing. 'And a man who wore a turban.'

'Ah, an Indian fellow, was it? He won't be hard to find. See anyone of that description hanging 'round, constable? Here now! Where is he?'

To our amazement, the doorway was empty. The officer had vanished!

'Why, he left his post without permission!' Lestrade exclaimed, with disbelief. 'In all my years, I've seen nothing like it. Mark my words, gentlemen, I shall have him on report for this!'

'A rather difficult task, I fear, Lestrade,' Holmes interjected, 'since I doubt if we shall ever see the man again. In fact, given his disappearance, I think we may safely conclude that he was no constable at all.'

'Oh, really now? What was he, then?'

Holmes's countenance turned grim. 'My executioner. His mission was to ascertain if Watson's bullet had done its work; if not, then to administer the *coup de grâce* himself, leaving the good doctor to shoulder the blame. An ingenious plan, you must admit. And but for you, Lestrade, it might very well have succeeded! For instead of finding Watson supine and only myself to dispose of, he was confronted by you, as well — a genuine policeman, with the very gun in his hand.'

'Good Lord!' I gasped, realising again how close it all had been. 'My dear Holmes, I don't know what to say! Can you ever forgive me? Obviously, somehow, I was in their power, but still — '

'My dear fellow!' Holmes assured me warmly, placing a sympathetic hand upon my shoulder. 'Cease your protestations! It is all behind us, now. And with nothing worse to show than that rather dark and peculiar hole in Mrs Hudson's ceiling. Are you feeling better? Would you care for a glass of brandy, perhaps? Good! Put up your feet, then, while I pour for us all, and we shall listen to whatever it is you can recollect.'

Unfortunately, there was not much. What had happened to me, or where I had ventured amidst the damp and snowy streets of London during the past few hours, remained for the most part a complete and utter mystery. I did, of course, remember purchasing my cigars — after which I spent a relaxing half-hour in the barber's chair, being ministered to for a haircut and shave. Thus trimmed and freshened, I had struck out south for exercise, in the direction of Hyde Park, towards Portman Square.

It was just after crossing Adam Street — where I was splattered and nearly struck down by a most discourteous four-wheeler — that I came upon a bereft and elderly fellow, crouching wearily in an alleyway. To my horror, as I passed by, the beggar uttered a groan and slumped heavily to the ground — clearly, it seemed to me, on his last legs!

Kneeling to help, my suspicions were confirmed — his complexion was pale and his breath, which reeked of spirits, was short. As I stood to call for a policeman, another man rushed up to lend a hand. 'Why, it's poor old Douglas!' he cried, cradling the tramp's head in his arm. 'Who of us hasn't said the bottle would get him yet?'

'Ah, you know him, then?' I enquired.

'I do,' the other replied. 'He needs his bed and a doctor's care, and not another pint!'

'Well, I am a doctor,' I informed him. 'Let's gather him up, then.'

'God bless you, sir. And I know his Martha will say the same. He lives not far from here, near Hertford House. We can save some time, if we cut back through this alley.' And so, off we went, slipping on the snowy cobblestones, as we carried the old vagrant between us.

'But you did not get far,' Holmes concluded, when I had told my tale.

'No. In fact, it was only moments later that I was grabbed and struck from behind.'

'And then?'

'After that, Holmes, I can remember little — until I awoke here to find you leaning over me. I feel certain that I was unconscious for a time — and yet, I wasn't! It was more as if I were in a daze. Everything in bits and pieces. Horses' hooves and water. Hands upon me. Voices. Darkness, light and darkness, and then something gleaming very bright. And, too — I swear! — I glimpsed a man who wore a turban. Close, and yet I could not see him clearly.'

'From what he says,' Lestrade observed, putting down his glass, 'You'd almost think he had been hypnotised. Not that I put much stock in all of that.'

'You should,' Holmes told him, 'now that you have seen it before your eyes.'

'Holmes, you mean that I — '

'You have been the victim of a very elaborate ruse, my dear Watson. You were waylaid, knocked senseless, and bundled into a cab. It was there, no doubt, the drug was administered, to prepare you for the hypnotist. An altered state of consciousness can be induced by a variety of methods. A gleaming object before the light is one.'

'Then you are saying Dr Watson was in a trance of sorts when he returned?' Lestrade suggested.

'A quite profound one. It is why he can remember so little of what transpired. Once in their power, he was given that gun, and ordered to use it, Lestrade. The sound of my voice, quite likely was what triggered his response.'

'Well, gentlemen, this is bizarre!' the policeman stated. 'Abduction and attempted murder, by a hypnotist and an accomplice, who impersonates an officer to boot. A very daring plan, to say the least! Have you that serious an enemy, then, Mr Holmes?'

'I have one. Professor Moriarty.'

'Moriarty!' I cried. 'Holmes, do you really believe I was in his awful clutches?'

Holmes nodded gravely. 'I do, Watson. Only he could have effected such a plan. He has the organisation and half a dozen dens along the river. Which, I suspect, is where you were taken, given the smells and sounds you have recounted.'

'If so, then what would be his motive?' Lestrade enquired. 'Revenge for the D'Arcy business, perhaps?'

'No, Lestrade, I think not. For Moriarty to have played this desperately, bigger stakes must be at hand. The monarchy, I am convinced, is not in danger. The question remains: what is? You must admit, this business of the runes has now taken on a completely different light.'

Lestrade appeared unconvinced. 'I don't know as I would go that far,' he remarked. 'For the life of me, I can see no connection.'

'Nor do I, at this moment,' Holmes admitted. 'And yet, can it be a mere coincidence that my life is thus attempted, so soon after these Crimson Vandals first appear?'

'You have a point,' Lestrade conceded. 'But why, then, did they wait a week? Monday or Tuesday, it seems to me, would have done them just as well.'

'Hardly. Watson, as I'm sure they've noticed, is an incurable creature of habit; he only walks on Saturday. It was the one time he could be absent for so long, without arousing my suspicions. Thus, an ideal time to strike.'

Holmes stood silently before the fire, contemplating matters for a moment, while he knocked the ashes from his black clay, then reached again for the Persian slipper.

'Moriarty knew, sooner or later, that you would come to me,' he told the policeman, pointedly, as he struck a match. 'Whatever his fiendish plan, he wanted to be certain I could not interfere.'

Lestrade sighed. It was clear, I could see, that he did not agree with my companion's feelings. 'Well,' he said officiously, rising from his chair, 'I must be off. Their Lordships await in Whitehall. Time will tell, I do expect, if Moriarty is involved. But frankly, Mr Holmes, I think you have him on the brain.'

'Do I? That is what MacDonald told me once, at the time of the Birlstone murder.[1] And I tell you now, Lestrade, that the subtle brushstrokes of Moriarty's

---

[1] *The Valley of Fear*, January 7–8, 1888.

work are as unmistakable today as they were then. These scribblings, I suspect, hold the answer to this business.'

'Well, you may keep them until Monday,' Lestrade replied. 'You will, I take it, keep me informed of whatever it is you might discover — Good day, then, gentlemen! And take care! Given what has happened here, I daresay you have good reason.'

No sooner had he gone than Holmes was tugging on his own coat and hat as well. After which he grabbed up the scrap of paper which Lestrade had left, and pocketed the small revolver from the top drawer of his desk.

'A wise precaution, I think,' he remarked, heading for the door. 'For once, Lestrade makes a good point; Moriarty may try again.'

'Why don't you take my Webley?' I suggested. 'Or better yet, I shall accompany you. You know the saying Holmes: 'A faithful friend is a strong defence'.'

Holmes paused at the doorway, a smile upon his face. 'And none more so than you, friend Watson! But no. Rest and gather your strength. I shall surely have need of your assistance before this matter is out. — Ah, but I must hurry! The museum closes at five; we have no time to waste.'

'It was awfully close,' I said.

'Extremely so. But we survived. And I'll tell you one thing, Watson. I would not want to be the Indian.'

★ ★ ★

The following day, a hastily scrawled message from Porlock confirmed what Holmes had suspected.

> The Indian is dead. Dropped through a trap door, hidden before M's desk. He is furious, afraid his latest scheme has been compromised. I dare not write more; his mood is foul today, and he watches us all quite closely. God help me if he discovers this.
>
> P.

It was not until many years later, when Porlock was able to surface after

Reichenbach, that we finally learned the chilling details of what had happened just hours after Holmes's close call — when the unfortunate Hindu was bound and taken to Moriarty's secret lair, hidden in a warehouse on the West India Docks, not far from the vile opium dens of Limehouse in London's East End.

The room into which the Indian was led was dark, save for a small lamp, which illuminated the top of Moriarty's desk. In its glow, only his pale, veined hands could be seen — nothing more. All was silent, save for the low rhythmic slapping of water against the building's foundation.

For an instant, Moriarty's left hand had disappeared from the light — then returned holding a small hourglass, which he set upon the desk.

'The sand in this will last for all of thirty seconds,' Moriarty said. His voice was soft, yet strangely terrifying. 'You have that long to tell me anything you wish to say.'

After which he turned the glass.

'But it was not my fault, Professor!' the

Indian cried. 'The trance worked perfectly. How could I know a policeman from Scotland Yard would be present?'

'It was a situation you should have allowed for. Oh, yes, you really should. Perhaps, for instance, you might have chosen a better time, or a different means.'

'But you must listen! It was the only time we had to lay our hands upon the doctor!' The Indian's eyes widened with fear, as he saw the sand slipping quickly downwards through the glass. 'Please, Professor! Give me another chance, I beg you! I will not fail, I swear — !'

Moriarty's left hand drew back, motioning for silence. 'What a shame. It is too late for that. Holmes now, you see, will surely be on his guard. Besides, I have other pressing matters in the next few days that require my full attention.'

The sand had run out. The top half of the hourglass was empty. Once again, Moriarty's left hand disappeared from the light.

'The point,' he said, 'is that I gave you an assignment. A rather simple errand, I felt — and you failed. You know my rules. There is only one punishment for that.'

Beneath the desk, Moriarty lightly fingered a small unseen button, located just below the drawer. The Indian was trembling now, so frightened he was unable to speak.

'Your hands and feet are bound, I see,' Moriarty observed. 'It will be difficult to swim, I imagine, tied together in that fashion.'

Desperately, the Indian strained against the ropes that held him. Unable to control himself any longer, he let out a cry of animal-like terror.

It was at that instant Moriarty pushed the button, which released a hidden spring. With a crash, the square of floor upon which the Indian stood gave way, and one last, hideous scream was heard, as he plunged into the cold, black waters below.

'What a pity,' Moriarty said, after a time. 'Sanders!'

'Yes, Professor?' the fake policeman asked.

'I am going to prove to you that I am a

188

generous man. You are forgiven for your part in this fiasco.'

The man stole a glance at the darkness that was behind him. 'Thank you, Professor.'

'Now, if you would, secure the trap door. And fetch me Langdon, as soon as possible. The painting has arrived; I shall have work for him to do.'

'You're going ahead with it, then?'

'I am. We can only hope that Holmes does not discover the true meaning of the Crimson Vandals. At least, not before Wednesday. Oh, my, no, that would never do.'

★ ★ ★

I had expected, when Holmes returned from the British Museum, that he would immediately closet himself with his findings and attempt to discern the meaning of the strange messages he possessed. Instead, while giving me a brief account of his earlier conversation with Lestrade, he quickly changed into one of his many disguises — this time, the grimy, worn attire of a common dock-hand — and went out again. As the evening passed, I began to worry; his destination, it seemed clear enough to me, had been the riverfront, and quite likely had something to do with Moriarty. At nine, feeling somewhat weary from the extraordinary events of the day, I suppressed my feelings of anxiety and took to my bed with a book and a glass of sherry. By eleven, when I caught myself nodding off and finally pinched out the candle, Holmes had still not returned.

On Sunday morning, when I came down about nine, I was surprised to find my friend working busily at his desk, clad in dressing gown and slippers, and sending up clouds of pale blue pipesmoke as he pored over sheets of crumpled foolscap and a large, dusty volume he had brought with him on his return from the museum. He had obviously risen early — if, indeed, he had been to bed at all — since the morning dailies were scattered haphazardly about his armchair, and his breakfast, I noted with disapproval, had clearly not been touched.

'My dear fellow,' I reminded him, 'you really should eat something! This habit of going without food for days is, I have no doubt, damaging to your system!'

Holmes made no reply. He was, I realised, so engrossed in his present task that he was oblivious to my presence. Knowing also his intense dislike of being interrupted from his reveries, I frowned but said nothing more, instead helping myself to the steaming coffee, eggs and ham which Mrs Hudson had supplied.

Approximately a half-hour later, after I had finished and was glancing at the *Times*, Holmes suddenly gave a cry of exaltation, put down his pen, and joined me at the table, filling his cup as well.

'Ah, Watson!' he exclaimed, stretching mightily, 'This has been a most productive morning.

As he reached across for the sugar, I noted with alarm a ragged cut across the back of his right hand.

'Holmes,' I cried, 'you're wounded. Not Moriarty, once again?'

'No, no, Watson. This trifle is the result of an argument over a game of darts, at an establishment called the Golden Swan, in Blackwall. It was all quite necessary, of course, to gain the confidence of the particular man I sought. Hah! Bother Lestrade and his police informants! A few hours inside a robbers' den, and I have learned more than they!'

'Well, pray then, tell me all. And while you do so I shall fetch my bag and administer to your hand.'

A moment later, when I returned, Holmes was still waiting restlessly at the table, drumming his long fingers nervously upon the cloth.

'Moriarty's alibi, as I suspected, is unassailable,' he informed me. 'On the afternoon my life was attempted, he was at the University Club in Cornwall, delivering a lecture on electrodynamics.'

'And how did you find that out?' I asked, as I brought forward warm water and bandages.

'A bit of information gleaned from an unsuspecting servant. You see, I had decided to watch Moriarty's house for a time, before I travelled to Blackwall. Alas, he was not at home.'

'Gone to ground, I would imagine. He probably fears retaliation.'

'Perhaps. At any rate, my contact at the Golden Swan provided me with some very interesting details — once I'd filled his hand with a pint and a half-sovereign. You were, of course, correct about the Indian. Moriarty has been seen in the company of a Hindu fellow of late; his name is Rajan-Raj. And, he has also added a known assassin to his payroll — 'Bloody' Jack Langdon is now in his employ.'

''Bloody' Jack, the knifeman?'

'The very one. An expert with both the stiletto and the throwing knife, at up to twenty paces. I also learned one other intriguing fact, Watson: Moriarty has engaged the services of a painter.'

'Painter? An artist, you mean?'

'Yes. Name of Joseph Potter. He has a small shop on Brook Street, not far from Stepney Station. I shall look him up tomorrow.'

'But what would Moriarty want with him?'

'The messages were meant to be found and read, Watson. In case you hadn't noticed, runes are hardly simple figures to reproduce. Moriarty would need someone with considerable skill to get them down at night, both accurately and quickly.'

My friend smiled faintly, with a look of satisfaction upon his face. 'Were Lestrade here now,' he added, 'I should tell him that is connection number one.'

'And number two?'

'I discovered it quite by chance, on my trip to the British Museum — which, I must say, was quite rewarding, thanks to the helpful clerk who supplied me with that most informative volume which now resides upon my desk. With it, and a few hours of honest cogitation, I have been able to decipher the cryptic messages.'

'Splendid!'

'To my good fortune, the clerk also possessed a memory keen as mustard. He recalled I was the second person within a month to enquire about runic scripture.'

'Oh?'

'The other,' Holmes said, 'was a scholarly gentleman named 'Mr Cornelius' — a tall, thin man with rounded shoulders.'

'Moriarty!'

Holmes smiled again, even as I applied the iodine. 'Precisely, Watson. Connection number two.'

'But what about the messages, Holmes? Whatever do they mean?'

'For the life of me, I must admit that I do not know.'

'But you said — !'

' — that I had deciphered them. And I have. Unfortunately, my good fellow, reading, as you shall see, is not always understanding. Finish up, now, and I shall show you where we stand.'

Moments later, Holmes began by arranging some sheets of his scribbling before me, atop his cluttered desk. 'This,' he said, indicating the first, 'is how the messages appeared after I had deciphered them. A rather easy task, since the book contains a detailed chart of Germanic, Anglo-Saxon and all other known runic forms. These runes are Northumberland, by the way, identifiable by the flagstaff mark which represents the letter 'a' — a symbol none of the other forms possess.'

For a moment I studied the lines before me:

ᛗᛁᚱᚱᛁᚱ ᛗᛂᛏ ᛋᛁᚢᛗᛒᛌᚱᚱ ᚼᛗᚱ
Elcric eht sla ec noc der

ᚼᛌᛁᛏ ᛗᛂᛏ ᚱᛁᛗᚱᛌᚱᚱ ᛋᛗᛗᚱᛏ ᛋᛁ
Dnal. eht lae cn oc seert sa

ᛗᚷᚼᛗᛁᛈᚱᛌᛚ ᚱᛁᛁ ᛋᛁᛁᛗᚱᛌᚱᚱ ᚼᛗᚱ
Egd elwo nk lla slaec noc d er

ᛋᚼᛌᛁᛏᛋ ᛂᛏᚱᚱᛏ ᚱᛁᛗᚱ ᛂᚱᛁᛈ ᚼᛌᛁᛂᛗᛒ
Sdn ats hturt laer hcihw dniheb

'But these lines make no sense at all,' I stated.

'Correct, Watson. That is because Moriarty added another little twist to his devious game — albeit a simple one.'

'And that was?'

'Merely to reverse the letters in each line.' Holmes pointed to the other sheet of foolscap. 'See here.'

This time, I read:

ᚱᛖᚻ   ᛒᚱᚩᚳᛖᚨᚠᚻ   ᛏᚩᛖ   ᚱᛁᚱᚱᛖᛗ
Red   conceals   the   circle

ᚾᚻ   ᛏᚱᛖᛖᚻ   ᛒᚱᚩᛖᛗᚱᛏ   ᛏᚩᛖ   ᚾᚱᛖᚻ
As   trees   conceal   the   land

ᚱᛖᚻ   ᛒᚱᚩᛖᛚᛖᚠᚻ   ᚾᛚᛏ   ᛁᚩᚱᛚᛖᚻᚷᛖ
Red   conceals   all   knowledge

ᛒᛖᛏᛁᚳᚻ   ᚠᛁᛁᚱᛏ   ᚱᛖᚱᛏ   ᛏᚱᚾᛏᛏ   ᚻᛏᚠᛏᚻᚻ
Behind   which   real   truth   stands

'Amazing, Holmes! Whatever made you think of that?'

'It is a common trick in cryptology, actually. So simple a ploy that I overlooked it at first, while I spent three-quarters of an hour trying one or two systematic codes instead. But come now, Doctor, tell me: what do you make of my discovery?'

'It's obviously some sort of verse,' I said. 'And I would guess it refers to the

197

Crimson Vandals, and something they are trying to conceal.'

'Excellent! Go on.'

'Well — outside of that, it tells me nothing.'

'On the contrary. It indicates quite clearly, I think, that these vandals will strike again soon. Twice more, if my reasoning is correct.'

'And how do you deduce that?'

'By the wording, Watson. It is just as obvious, you must admit, that the verse is not complete. Hence, more acts of vandalism will follow — until, as I suspect, we have received the entire passage. Now metre hints at a six- or eight-line axiom; my guess is six. That means they will appear at least twice again.'

'But is there nothing we can do?' I asked, desperation creeping into my voice.

'My dear fellow, what would you suggest? Post a constable beside every statue and graveyard in the city?' Holmes returned his attention once more to the four lines which lay before him. 'No, I'm afraid we're stalemated, at the moment — unless I can somehow solve this puzzle.'

It was at that moment that Mrs Hudson appeared, bearing an envelope which had, she told us, been left upon our doorstep some time before. Inside was the aforementioned message of doom from Porlock.

Upon reading it, I had that same uneasy feeling as I had experienced on the morning of my regiment's advance upon Maiwand — that even worse trouble was ahead.

In spite of the early hour, I poured myself a stiff glass of Pattisons, leaving Holmes to his pipe and deductive thoughts before our hearty fire. Parting the curtains, I glanced down into the street. It was snowing lightly, once again.

* * *

We had not long to wait. A quarter past seven the following morning, a weary Lestrade was at our door, bringing news that fresh developments were at hand.

That he had been up for quite some time was evident; both his haggard face and the dark circles beneath his eyes spoke of little sleep.

'I was out before daylight this morning, gentlemen,' he told us, as we all partook of coffee. 'It has been a busy night. Affairs have taken a graver turn, I'm afraid. The Crimson Vandals have struck again. And there's been a murder in Stepney.'

'Stepney!' I burst out, recalling Holmes's mention of the artist Moriarty had employed. 'Who was the victim?'

'An art dealer by the name of Peter Jacobsen. He lived above his shop in Abbott's Lane. During the night, there was a break-in; robbery, I suspect. Jacobsen apparently surprised the thief — and paid for it with his life.'

'How was he killed?' Sherlock Holmes enquired.

'He was stabbed to death. A clean job, I must say. One wound under the rib cage, straight into the heart.'

Holmes and I exchanged a glance.

'And the Vandals?' Holmes asked. 'Where this time?'

'Trafalgar Square,' Lestrade said, with a sigh. 'They painted the head of George IV, bloody red as you please.'

'There was a message?'

'Yes. But I didn't have time to copy it down. I had only arrived at the scene, when I was summoned to Abbott's Lane. However, I did as you requested: there's a cordon of constables all round, with orders that nothing be disturbed.'

'Excellent!' Holmes cried, leaping eagerly to his feet. An excited gleam was in his gimlet eyes, and at that instant he reminded me much of a hound who has just been given the scent. 'We shall look things over there, and then be off to Stepney.'

'You speak as if there were some connection,' Lestrade suggested, as we grabbed our coats and hats. 'Apparently you know something I do not. Gleaned from those messages, I suppose?'

'Unfortunately, no,' my friend replied. 'But come! I shall explain all, once we're in your carriage.'

Light flakes of snow were gently falling as we climbed into our conveyance, and our breath showed white before us in the winter air. As we passed through the snowy streets of London making our way south towards Piccadilly, Holmes related to Lestrade what we had learned: the cryptic poem hidden in the runic messages, the ghastly demise of the turbaned man, as well as Moriarty's reported hiring of both the artist, Joseph Potter, and 'Bloody' Jack, the knifeman.

'By George!' Lestrade exclaimed, when Holmes had finished. 'Given all that, I think I shall have a talk with this Moriarty fellow myself, once we're through. I should be interested in hearing what he has to say.'

Holmes frowned with displeasure. 'I'd rather you didn't, Lestrade,' he cautioned. 'After all, you have no proof — only conjecture, and rumour second-hand. Besides, why sound the alarm so soon? The wolf is much more wary when he knows a hunter is near.'

The policeman paused, to mull matters for a second or two.

'Very well,' he conceded. 'I shall take your advice for now. But given the way Jacobsen met his end, I am issuing a warrant for 'Bloody' Jack.'

Because of the snow the heavy traffic was slower than usual at Piccadilly Circus, causing us some delay as our cab crossed the busy circle. That done, however, we were able to make our way south on the Haymarket at a remarkably brisk clip, and were soon passing the tall, white columns of the celebrated theatre itself. At Pall Mall, we turned east, and moments later alighted in front of the National Gallery, overlooking Trafalgar Square.

My first thought, as I felt the crunch of snow beneath my shoes, was to pause at the rail and reflect a moment upon the majestic beauty of the winter scene that was spread before us. Amidst the swirling flakes, life in London went on as usual, as hundreds of hardy souls were making their way back and forth across the gigantic, snow-covered square, intent on completing their appointed errands, no matter what the weather. From atop their pedestals, the bronze statues of Havelock and Napier serenely watched this industrious ebb and flow of humanity, as did

Landseer's four huge lions, which had guarded Nelson's Column for the past two decades. Glancing up at the cold, grey sky, I could just glimpse the stone likeness of England's greatest admiral himself, standing alone on his towering shaft of Devonshire granite, more than one hundred feet above us.

Our attention, however, was quickly attracted to a crowd that had gathered at the northeast corner of the square, towards which we now made our way. The object of interest, I could plainly see, was the equestrian statue of King George IV, which stood next to the wide, concrete staircase that connected the street to the square below.

Anger welled inside my chest, as we drew near. The noble features of the man known as 'the first gentleman of Europe' had been besmirched in red.

'Well, I never — ' I began.

'Here, now! Let us through!' Lestrade barked out, as he wedged his way into the throng. 'This is official police business! Step aside!'

Moments later we stood inside a

resolute circle of London's finest, who had kept the crowd back for some twenty feet. How the Vandals had accomplished their task seemed easy enough to see: A twelve-foot workman's ladder had been left standing against the statue's concrete pedestal, and there were clearly footmarks in the snow. Across the back of the pedestal, about shoulder high, the tell-tale line of runic figures had been painted:

ᛏᛉᚠ ᚻᛁ ᛏᛈᚻᚦ ᚻᛁ

ᚻᛡᛈᚻ ᚺᛗᚱ ᚦᛏᚢᚱᛏ

'The ladder is an interesting point,' Lestrade remarked. 'I suspect they were surprised, somehow, and were unable to carry it off.'

'Either that,' Holmes mused, as he glanced about, 'or they had no further use for it. My compliments, Lestrade. Your men seem to have kept this area well protected. With your permission?'

'By all means.'

Holmes whipped out his glass and proceeded to examine the indentations in the snow, delicately stepping this way and that, so as not to disturb a thing. That done, he nimbly climbed atop the concrete rail that overlooked the square, and carefully stepped his way along it until he reached the point where the railing met the pedestal's base, some four feet off the ground. Then, to my amazement, he swung himself gently out onto the ladder, and, feeling it secure, edged cautiously up one more step, peering at something intently.

'You must admit,' Lestrade observed, 'that getting up there was a tricky business.'

'I think not. I am hardly acrobatic, Lestrade, yet I have no doubt, should you secure the ladder, that I could easily clamber up beside the good King's horse with paint in hand. A simple hook and rope would suffice to join him in the saddle. It could all be done, I imagine, in about ten minutes' time.'

As gracefully as he had risen, my friend eased himself off the ladder and back onto the rail, retraced his steps along it, and then hopped down beside us in the street.

'By the footmarks, I would say there were three men,' he stated. 'One who held the ladder, one who climbed it, and one who left the message. A fourth, I imagine, kept watch some distance away. The man who held the ladder was approximately six feet tall and obviously strong. He also smokes; a cigarette has been crushed at the base of the ladder. By their stride, I'd say the other two men were shorter. The circular marks in the snow next to the pedestal show where they set their lantern, and two small pots of paint.'

'Splendid, Holmes!' I effused. 'Why, you have re-created it all perfectly!'

'One other point of significance,' Holmes added, 'is that the initials 'E.B.' are carved into the ladder, just below the topmost rung.'

'You don't say?' Lestrade remarked, glancing up from his notebook, in which he was scribbling furiously. 'And what of this latest scrawl, Mr Holmes? You are more familiar with these runes than I.'

Taking the policeman's pad and pencil, Holmes studied the markings for a time, transcribing them into a row of letters on the page. After which, he transposed the last to first, and so on, until the reversal of the entire line was complete. The result, which he held before us in the lightly falling snow, was this:

Truth, red says, is what is not

For a moment, we all stared silently down at that intriguing scrap of paper, each, I felt, thinking our particular thoughts about what the line could mean, as well as those which had proceeded it.

'This tells us nothing more than we knew before,' I stated, finally, unable to hide my disappointment. 'It's obvious these Vandals are a screen for some other act, or crime. But what?'

Lestrade rubbed his chin thoughtfully. 'What, indeed,' he said. 'I'll tell you one thing, Doctor. If what Mr Holmes tells us is true, I'd give a fortnight's pay to see that final line.'

'Oh, you shall,' Holmes assured him.

'But by then, I fear, all will be too late. Come. Perhaps something will turn our way in Stepney.

★ ★ ★

Peter Jacobsen's small art store was located on the corner of a rather nondescript, aged brick building, one of many such plain structures which lined the snowy street called Abbott's Lane. In spite of nature's soft white covering, it seemed a dreary venue, an endless hodgepodge of grimy shop windows, advertising posters and frontages sorely in need of a coat of paint. To the left, Jacobsen's establishment was buttressed by something called 'The British School of Monitoring'; to the right was a small alleyway, which led to the rear of the building. As we alighted, I noted a few people had already gathered in the street — curious, no doubt, at seeing the black police van outside, and two uniformed constables at Jacobsen's door. Given the grim reason for our visit, the two bright landscapes on display in the dealer's front window seemed grotesquely out of place.

Holmes paused before the door. 'Who discovered the body?' he asked.

'I did, sir,' the nearest constable answered. 'It was a bit after four; I was making my normal round.'

'And what did you see?'

'Footsteps in the snow, sir. And this door open, just a crack. At first I thought perhaps it was forgetfulness — you know, a toff home late with a drop too much to drink. But then, I had this feeling. So I stepped inside, and flashed my light about, and called up the stairs at the back. When I got no answer, I went on up — and found 'im dead for sure, lying on his back.'

Holmes knelt down and examined the keyhole of the door closely with his glass.

'This is interesting,' he said. 'There's not a mark upon it. Not a scratch upon the ward, where pressure would have been applied.'

Lestrade jumped like a cat upon a mouse. 'Well, if entry was not forced,' he declared, 'then it's certainly simple enough. Either Jacobsen knew his killer, and let him in, or the killer had a key.'

Holmes said nothing, and stepped inside.

We followed Lestrade to the rear of Jacobsen's crowded shop, past displays of oils and watercolours depicting various, time-honoured themes: forested landscape, young girls swinging gaily in a park, bright-coloured birds perched alertly above a stream, large bowls of gleaming fruit. (At the thought of food, my stomach growled, reminding me that I had not had breakfast.) Jacobsen, I noted as we passed the counter, had sold art supplies as well: his shelves were stocked with brushes, tubes of paint, palettes and boxes of coloured charcoals and chalks. Blank canvasses and empty frames lay stacked against the wall.

Lestrade then led us up a flight of stairs, to Jacobsen's living quarters. Holmes, I noticed as we progressed, paused once or twice to press the boards with his bare hand. At the top of the stairs was a window on our left and a long hallway to the right. Two doors were visible, and a burly constable standing beside the first.

'Jacobsen lived here,' Lestrade explained. 'The other door leads to a storage room. I have already examined it; nothing appears to be missing.'

Holmes stepped to the window, and examined the latch.

'Locked, as you can see,' Lestrade commented. 'As was the door leading to the alley. This way.'

'How many people have entered this room?' Holmes asked, as Lestrade swung open the door. At first glance, the flat appeared plain enough, a small kitchen, table and chairs, and a sleeping area at the rear, which had been partitioned off by a curtain. Next to the bed, a bureau drawer hung open, and two objects lay upon the floor — a metal cashbox, empty save for a few odd shillings, and a small candle in its stand.

'Why, no one. Save myself, and the constable who originally happened on the scene.'

'Good. Then, with your permission, we shall have a look about. Watson, if you would — the body?'

Peter Jacobsen was lying on his back in

the middle of the room, dressed only in his nightclothes, his dead eyes staring vacantly at the ceiling. Just below his rib cage, and slightly to the left, a dark circle of blood had soaked through the material and coagulated. Rigor mortis had set in.

'A powerful man did this, Holmes,' I said, as we knelt beside the inert form. 'You see how the wound is jagged at the edges? The blade was clearly pushed from side to side repeatedly, after the initial thrust, to cause maximum damage. By the condition of the body, I'd say death occurred some time after midnight.'

'And the angle of the wound?'

'An upward thrust, certainly. An examination, I'm certain, will show the blade mortally pierced the heart. Death was almost instantaneous.'

Holmes whipped out his glass, and began to crawl about on his hands and knees, in an ever-widening circle around the body. Then, while Lestrade and I watched silently, he examined the entire area, carpet and floorboards, from the victim's outstretched feet to the doorway, and out into the hall.

It was then I heard his yelp of triumph.

'What did you find, Holmes?' I asked.

'What I had hoped for, Watson. Candle wax.'

Lestrade snorted. 'Wax, indeed!' he said, as Holmes continued his investigations in the hall. 'Why, what happened here is clear enough to see! The thief entered this room and began his search, which woke poor Jacobsen from his bed. Before he could manage to strike a light, the man was on him! They struggled, and he stabbed him here. After that, the thief lit that candle, found the money, and fled back down to the street. Have I missed anything, Mr Holmes?'

'Except for the quite obvious fact that Jacobsen's moneybox has been emptied,' Holmes replied, as he re-entered the room. 'I conclude you have missed it all. Now — would you be so kind as to accompany us to the alley?'

As we stepped down off the kerb, Holmes cautioned us to walk behind him, pointing out two sets of footprints in the snow. 'You'll note both were made by the same set of shoes, Lestrade,' my friend remarked, as we carefully made our way. 'Also, that both sets head in the same direction. The second, however, which at times covers the first, is spaced much further apart. It is, you must admit, most suggestive.'

Lestrade said nothing. He was, I could see, still smarting from Holmes's rebuff inside.

In the alleyway behind the building, Holmes noted a set of wheelmarks, which, along with the two sets of footprints, we followed until we stood at the rear of Jacobsen's store.

Holmes glanced about, a look of satisfaction on his lean face.

'Thanks to Mother Nature, it is all before us,' he said. 'Why, they could not have done better had they left a map! The first set of prints, you see, follows the cart down the alley, then walks to the other side, while the cart waited here — you see where the horse's hooves crushed down the snow? Then our man recrossed the alley, and placed his ladder under Jacobsen's window — '

'Ladder — !' Lestrade ejaculated.

'Yes. That window is where the murderer entered, not the shop door from the street.'

Before Holmes could continue further, we heard the harsh scrape and creak of a door opening behind us. Turning round, we saw a bearded fellow peeking out from his back step across the alley.

'Hello,' he said. 'Are you the police?'

'We are,' Lestrade said. 'Why do you ask?'

'Because I wish to issue a complaint. Someone has stolen my ladder.'

'Oh, really?'

'Yes. I placed it against this wall last night, before I retired to bed. And this morning I found it gone.'

'Would it be a twelve-footer?' Holmes enquired. 'With your initials carved inside the rail?'

'Yes, sir!' the man fairly beamed. 'You've found it, then?'

'That depends. What is your name and occupation?'

'Biggle, sir. Edward Biggle. I'm a mason, and when things are slow, I wash windows for Mayhew & Gardner's. That's why I need the ladder, sir. I've got a job today.'

Holmes chuckled. 'Well, take heart, then, Edward Biggle. This is Inspector Lestrade of Scotland Yard. Thanks to his abundant perspicacity, your ladder is already in the hands of the police.'

Holmes turned on his heel and strode jauntily off, leaving Lestrade to fume again.

'If you check the hall window carefully,' Holmes explained, as we retraced our steps to the street, 'you will find the latch is sprung. The window was forced, then locked again, so it would not attract attention. There are, however, blade marks upon the outside sill, and the snow has been disturbed in three places upon the ledge.

'The killer, I have no doubt, entered there. And, upon hearing Jacobsen approach, waited in the shadow by the staircase. When the unfortunate man stepped out, he grabbed him from behind and thrust home the knife, killing him on the spot.'

'And how can you prove that?' Lestrade

enquired, this time without the sarcasm.

'Candle wax, Inspector. When the killer grabbed Jacobsen, he surely dropped his candle. Yet there were no drops of wax beside the body. You will, however, find them on the floor-boards in the hall. A close inspection of the carpeting also showed the line of the victim's heelmarks, made when his body was dragged into the room. After establishing robbery as the motive, the killer left through the front door of the store, making sure it was left open, and returned to the alley. He was in a hurry this time, which is why the second set of footprints are a bit further apart. After all, he and his confederates still had a visit to pay to the statue of George IV.'

'All well and good, Holmes,' I concurred. 'But why, then, was Jacobsen killed? And why bother to conceal where the killer entered the building? It doesn't seem to matter to me.'

'My dear Watson!' Holmes exclaimed, as we turned the corner on to the street. 'Don't you see? The answer to one question is the answer to the other. I can only hope we find that answer inside.'

Upon re-entering the art dealer's shop, Holmes began to slowly pace about, examining this and that, taking in all that was before him. As he stepped behind the counter, he suddenly knelt down and pressed his palm against the floor. 'Another suggestive point,' he said. 'These boards, like the stairs, are still quite damp. Yet elsewhere about the counter, there is no evidence of heavy traffic.'

'Which means?'

'That someone stood in this particular spot for quite some time, Watson. Someone whose shoes were wet.'

'Perhaps it was the killer, seeking money from the register,' Lestrade suggested.

'Or someone else, seeking this?' From beneath the counter, Holmes produced a small brown ledger, which he began to pore over intently, running his long index finger up and down the pages. 'Let's see, sales on the left, purchases on the right — Hello! What's this?'

Next to his finger, under 'Items Sold', were written the words: Velvet Vision, J. Potter, 10/6.

'Good Lord!' I exclaimed. 'Joseph Potter, Moriarty's artist! So they knew each other, then?'

'For quite some time. The sale of Potter's painting is dated August the seventh. Actually, I'm not surprised; Brook Street is only a few streets away.'

'Holmes, do you think it was Jacobsen who introduced Moriarty to Potter?' I asked.

My friend gave me a quizzical look. 'Or,' he replied, evenly, 'was it the other way around?'

Furiously, Holmes continued to comb the pages, until suddenly he uttered a cry of despair. Before us was the final page of recorded entries, covering transactions Jacobsen had made in recent weeks. On the left side under 'Items Sold', three lines were written. The right half had been torn away.

'This,' Holmes said, 'explains it.'

Lestrade and I exchanged a glance. What Holmes was driving at, neither of us could clearly fathom.

'My dear fellow,' I enquired, 'whatever do you mean?'

'Don't you see, Watson? It all fits. Potter introduced Moriarty to Jacobsen, in order that he could make a purchase for him. A purchase Jacobsen duly recorded in this ledger. That is what Moriarty wished to conceal. It is the reason Jacobsen was killed, and why great pains were taken to make it appear a thief had entered from the street.'

'Then you think the killer removed this page, after he stabbed Jacobsen?' Lestrade asked.

'No. After all, he had other business awaiting him at Trafalgar Square. Besides, this was too important an errand to be trusted. My guess is that the killer — Langdon — hurried down and let Moriarty himself in through the front. After which, he returned again to the alley.'

'Well, given the dead man's profession,' I speculated, 'it seems safe to assume he secured a painting for Moriarty. Now if we only had some way of knowing what it was — '

'Perhaps we do,' Holmes replied. He removed a small card which had been inserted face down in the spine of the ledger. The inscription read:

        Claude Jarre
        Objets d'Art
        40 Blvd des Chenes
        Calais

'A stroke of luck, indeed!' Holmes intoned. 'In the half-light, Moriarty must not have noticed, in his haste.'

'But, Holmes,' I insisted, 'that card might not have anything to do with Moriarty's purchase. It could, for example, refer to any of these three items that are listed.'

'It is not likely, Watson. All are inexpensive, priced at ten pounds or less. It would hardly be worth Jacobsen's while to seek out a dealer on the Continent, unless the consignment were valuable enough to assure a healthy fee. Flip back through these pages, and I doubt if you'll find a handful thus, during the past two years. No, this card concerns Moriarty, and what he sought — of that, I'm certain.'

'And what do you propose to do?' Lestrade enquired. 'It's clear to me that Langdon is our man.'

'I have two leads, at present,' Holmes replied, ignoring Lestrade's remark. 'Joseph Potter, and the card of Monsieur Jarre. I shall spend my afternoon attempting to locate the former; if I fail, the latter shall accompany me to Calais.'

* * *

When Holmes returned to our lodgings at Baker Street at approximately half past five, I could tell immediately by his downcast expression that the day had not gone well — which meant, of course, that he had been unable to discover the whereabouts of the elusive artist, Joseph Potter.

'It's as if the man had vanished from the face of the earth, Watson!' he declared, as he threw off his coat and hat. 'Is there possibly a glass of Tokay about? This has been a frustrating day. Ah, well, perhaps young Wiggins will have good news for us. I've told him to report to me here at six.'

'No news, more likely,' I muttered, as I poured him the requested wine. 'Holmes, why do you insist on retaining those grimy urchins, anyhow? As I see it, you're throwing good money after bad.'

Holmes clucked his tongue disapprovingly, as he sank back into his favourite armchair, tobacco and pipe in hand. 'Now, now, Watson,' he chided, as he proceeded to fill the bowl with shag. 'Let's not be uncharitable. You must admit, those ragamuffins have done us more than one good turn in the past.'

Holmes referred, of course, to the Baker Street Irregulars, a group of unsavoury street arabs he had recruited some years back for searching the streets of London. His idea being that, unlike any member of the official force, the rag-tag boys could go everywhere, see everything, and overhear anyone — all without the slightest suspicion. Two of his more notable successes (dutifully recorded in previous cases) were in locating the cabbie, Jefferson

Hope,[1] and the steam launch *Aurora*.[2] However, at a shilling each per day, I felt the unwashed vagabonds were horrendously overpaid.

'I am well aware that these children have been helpful — on occasion,' I replied, as I joined him before the fire. 'But from a practical standpoint, I view their infrequent services as highly over-priced.'

Holmes seemed amused. 'A Scotsman's opinion, no doubt,' he said.

I frowned. My first thought was a tart reply, but my intense curiosity concerning his whereabouts overruled my pique. 'Perhaps,' I conceded. 'But come now, tell me: What have you been up to these past hours?'

Holmes savoured a taste of the sweet, Hungarian grape, then lit his pipe and inhaled deeply, causing small clouds of smoke to emanate from his black clay.

---

[1] *A Study in Scarlet*, March 4–7, 1881.

[2] *The Sign of Four*, September 18–21, 1888.

'My travels,' he began, 'took me first to Brook Street, where with some help from Inspector Lestrade we were able to persuade Potter's landlady to allow us to inspect his flat. I had hoped it would provide a wealth of clues, Watson — you know how untidy those Bohemian types can be! Alas, however, our search revealed little, save for one intriguing fact: according to a passbook I discovered, our struggling artist recently opened an account at Barclay's on the tenth, depositing no less than one hundred pounds!'

'Whew!' I whistled. 'Surely, none of his paintings are worth a fraction of that.'

'My thoughts, exactly. I suspect, instead, that it was a payment in advance for services rendered — from our old friend the professor. The clerk at Barclay's recalled that the deposit was in cash.'

'What of the landlady? Was she of any help?'

'Not much. She told us she had last seen Potter on Saturday evening — '

'The day your life was attempted!' I

burst forth, immediately regretting I had done so. Embarrassed, I glanced away.

'Precisely, Watson. It only confirms to me that Potter, upon orders from Moriarty, has been in hiding ever since. The landlady also told us Potter had few visitors, save for an older sister who lived in Chiswick; she gave me her address. So off I went to Chiswick, in the guise of a solicitor.'

'A solicitor? Whatever for?'

'To plant a seed I hope will germinate.'

'A seed? I'm sorry, Holmes, but I do not follow you at all.'

'Well, since the two are close, might not Potter visit her sometime soon? There are worse places to hide than Chiswick; it is off the beaten track. Should Potter decide to do so, I have left some bait.'

'Bait now, is it!' I said. 'Holmes, will you come to the point?'

My companion chuckled, allowing himself another sip of wine. 'My dear fellow,' he said, 'what better lure is there to someone down and out than the thought of sudden wealth? I merely informed the woman that I represented one Thurgood Potter of Folkestone, recently deceased, and that she and her brother had both been named in the will. I told her it was a matter of several thousand pounds, to be divided equally, but that the papers required both their signatures before either could collect.'

'And what was her reaction?'

'Suspicion, until I showed her a document attesting to the fact, signed and dated.'

'But how — ?'

'An easy ruse, Watson. It is a standard document I had purchased from an agent, and filled in myself while I was riding on the train. I told her she and her brother could contact me at this address. It is a bit of a long shot, I admit, but we do not have many cards which we can play — '

Holmes paused at the sound of footsteps on the stair. 'That will be Wiggins,' he said. I knew that he had recognised the tread. 'Ah, and prompt as well, if we are to believe our mantle clock. Show him in, will you, Watson?'

A moment later, the scruffy young

beggar stood before us, as smudged and unwashed as ever, wearing a shabby checked coat and woollen scarf, his crumpled cloth cap in his hand. By his flushed cheeks and wet shoes, I surmised that he had just spent many hours prowling the streets of the city, despite the adverse elements. It was, I realised guiltily, a mean way to earn a shilling.

Regretting my earlier remarks, I decided to offer the lad my chair before the fire, but Holmes, as usual, was a step ahead in his observations. Taking Wiggins by the elbow, he guided him to his seat, then proceeded to pour him a steaming cup of tea.

'Well, Wiggins,' he asked, 'have you found our man?'

'No, sir,' the boy replied. 'We hain't. But I can tell you where he's laid up the past few days.'

'And where is that?'

'A room on Butcher Row, sir — that is, 'til this morning. The bloke left quick, and stiffed 'em for a florin, Sticker says.'

'Sticker?' I enquired.

The urchin grinned, revealing a set of

yellowed teeth, and a space where one was missing.

'Ay, sir! My best man, 'e is! Sticks around longer than most, you know? An' he's got a way about 'im, Sticker has. People likes to tell 'im things.'

Holmes drew deeply on his pipe. 'I doubt if our man has flown,' he concluded, darkly. 'After all, his business with Moriarty is not finished. More likely, he has been ordered to stay on the move. Now then, Wiggins. Where did your band get to today?'

'We worked south from Stepney Station towards the Basin, sir, jes' like you told us. But where this fly'll light tomorrow is anybody's guess.'

Holmes reached into his pocket for some coins, and handed the lad six shillings. This meant, I knew, that he desired the search to be continued, since he always paid the urchins in advance. 'My suspicion, Wiggins,' he said, 'is that he'll travel east, perhaps as far as Limehouse. Moriarty, I have heard, has a lair there. — Oh, and send one boy the other way to Chiswick! Here's the address, and an extra three shillings for expenses. Tell him to be sharp, and follow the woman who lives there, should she decide to leave.'

'Good 'nuf, sir.' Rising, the grimy child tugged on his cap, and headed for the door. 'And thanks t' you, for the char.'

For some moments after Wiggins had gone, I sat silently before the fire, contemplating the considerable task his band of gritty gypsies faced. London, after all, was a huge metropolis; the odds of locating one man among its teeming millions seemed immense.

'I hate to be a doomsayer, Holmes,' I said, at last, 'but do you really think it possible they will find Potter? The prospects, to me, seem rather bleak. I mean, it's not as if he were an acrobat in a circus, and you had only to post a watch at centre ring.'

My companion's reaction to my words was nothing I could have imagined. For a moment, he stared at me fixedly, then leapt suddenly to his feet. 'My God!' he cried, slapping his hand upon his head. 'Why did I not think of it before? Why, I spoke the very word myself at Trafalgar Square!'

'Word? Holmes, what — ?'

'Acrobat, Watson! Don't you see! As you suggested, Potter is no acrobat. But what of the other man, who swung so easily atop King George's horse, with paint and brush in hand? If Moriarty could hire both an artist and assassin, then why not someone who was quick upon his feet?' He rushed to his desk, took up pen and paper, and began to scribble feverishly.

'What are you doing?' I asked.

'I am writing a telegram, to an old friend,' he replied. 'I am in hopes he will help us find our gymnastic brushman.'

'And who, pray tell, is that?'

Holmes smiled faintly. 'Come, come, Watson. You said yourself that all we need do was stand by centre ring. I am merely writing to the man who owns the most successful centre ring in England.'

'Lord George Sanger!' I burst forth. 'The showman?'

'Who else? It is the dead of winter, after all, and his is the only circus in London.

We shall visit him on the morrow, at Astley's on Westminster.'

* * *

The happenstances of life have never ceased to intrigue me. Thus, I was struck by the fact that had Phillip Astley not helped George III subdue a spirited horse near Westminster Bridge in 1769 we should not have found ourselves alighting from a hansom in front of Sanger's Grand National Amphitheatre, shortly before nine the following morning.

'The monarch was so grateful,' I said, as I mentioned it to Holmes, 'that he granted Astley both the land and licence to perform. It was, I read somewhere, a horse show under a simple canvas tent in the beginning.'

'I was not aware the circus, or Astley's, held such interest for you, Watson,' Holmes remarked, as he stepped down into the street. Like most Londoners, he still referred to it as Astley's, even though Sanger had officially changed the name when he bought the giant showplace in 1871.

'I have always enjoyed the circus,' I rejoined. 'Why, my father took me to see Mazeppa's Rise,[1] when I was eight. Holmes, did you know this building has been destroyed by fire three times? Yet, here we are more than a century later, and the circus is still with us, upon this very spot.'

Holmes clapped me heartily upon the shoulder. 'My dear Watson,' he said, 'I do declare! You are the very soul of English continuity and tradition. As long as stalwart fellows like yourself abound, the Empire, like the show, will most certainly go on!'

That our arrival had been anticipated was clearly evident, when at the side door, Holmes had merely to mention his

---

[1] A romantic tale, featuring horseback riding, which was highly popular throughout England in the early 1800s. Watson, no doubt, saw Mazeppa performed at a County Fair in his rural Scotland somewhere in the vicinity of Stranraer.

name, and we were quickly and graciously escorted inside to the office of a Mr Andrew Oliver, business manager for Sanger's 'London and Continental Circus'. He, in turn, guided us through a series of shadowy corridors and archways which led to the private sanctum of Sanger himself. As our footsteps echoed through the empty hallways, I felt a growing sense of expectation about meeting this man who, seventeen years before, had restored success to what was then a dying structure, and then proceeded to estab- lish well-received circuses in Islington, Manchester, Liverpool, and many other cities as well. As to what Holmes's previous involvement with Sanger had been, however, I could not dare to guess.

Before I had time to speculate further, we paused at a heavy, oaken door, upon which Oliver registered two light taps.

'Who is it?' a voice enquired, from within.

'Oliver, sir. With Mr Sherlock Holmes and Dr Watson.'

From behind the door, we heard the

scrape of a chair, footsteps and a low metallic sound. Then after a moment, a bolt was pushed back, the heavy door swung open, and Sanger stood before us.

'Sherlock Holmes!' he cried, pumping my friend's hand. 'It has been too many years! — And you, sir, must be Dr Watson!' he added, doing the same to mine. 'Come in, gentlemen! Do come in!'

We followed our host into the room, whose walls were decorated with bright-coloured advertising bills and other circus tokens, mementoes of shows long past. While Sanger was not a large man, he cut an imposing figure, elegantly dressed in black trousers and elastic side boots, a ruffled white silk shirt, and a black satin tie in which was nestled the sparkling, jewelled pin that had, I recalled, once been presented him by the Queen. His coal-black hair, moustache and eyebrows only added to the dashing effect.

'I received your telegram, Mr Holmes,' the showman said, as he motioned us to our chairs. 'You stated you wished my assistance, in a rather delicate affair. Said is done for you, my friend! Was there any doubt you would receive it?'

Both the depth and sincerity of Sanger's words caught me by surprise. And, of course, left me more curious than ever as to what had passed between these two remarkable men.

'None, whatsoever,' my friend assured him, warmly. 'However, Mr Sanger, I fear the timing of our visit inopportune. You were, I gather, preparing to depart for Cox & Co., in order to make a quite large deposit?'

For an instant, the circus master, like myself, sat taken aback. Then, with a hearty laugh, he proclaimed his admiration. 'Lord above, Mr Holmes!' he declared. 'You read my very mind! Is there nothing, save the powers that be, that you cannot decipher? How were you aware that I planned to call upon the bank? And who informed you of my financial circumstances?'

'Why, you did, Lord George.'

'What — ?'

Holmes gestured slightly, as if to signify to Sanger, as he had so often to me, that the matter was a simple one. 'My conclusion is easily drawn,' he stated. 'According to your bill, the London and Continental performed last night, and there is not another show 'til Thursday. Thus, heavy money must lie about. And when I find you closeted behind a bolted door of heavy oak, I divine it must be here. A safe in that small closet, perhaps? Or beneath your desk? I am certain I heard it clang shut, after you had risen from your chair.'

Sanger eyed Holmes shrewdly. 'And what if I was to tell you that the money had already been despatched?' he asked.

'Why, then I simply would not believe you!' Holmes declared, with some amusement. The two, I could tell, had squared off this way before. 'If the money were gone, why bother to bolt the door, or close the safe at all? Besides, unless I am mistaken, that is a deposit book from Cox's Charing Cross branch, lying next to your hat and stick. I seriously doubt that you would send a messenger without it.'

Sanger threw up his hands. 'Splendid!' he cried. 'Why, Mr Holmes, you are still as sharp as glass! Sharp as when you were Grimaldi the Illusionist, eh? — Now that, Dr Watson, was an episode truly worthy of your well-known journalistic talents.'

I could not hide my amazement. So Holmes had actually performed, in disguise, in one of Sanger's circuses! And, given Sanger's allusive remark, solved some sort of mystery for his employer.

'Holmes, you never — !' I began.

'It was before your time, Watson; an unpleasant business, to be sure! With Lord George's permission, I shall give the particulars later. Suffice to say, it concerned the untimely and violent death of Palmyra, an accomplished female aerialist — '

' — And nearly cost me my show and reputation!' Sanger said. 'Were it not for your cunning, Mr Holmes, I seriously doubt if I should find myself in the grandiose position I am today. — But come, gentlemen, enough of the past. You seek my help, Mr Holmes, and I am quite prepared to give it. Tell me what you wish.'

'You are familiar with the recent

crimes of the Crimson Vandals?' Holmes enquired.

'I am! The despicable curs! That any British subject could commit such acts, gentlemen, is quite beyond my contemplation! When they are caught, and I am confident they shall be, the deepest cell in Newgate Prison should serve as their reward.'

Holmes looked at the irate showman (who was well known for his patriotism) squarely in the eye. 'I have reason to believe,' he told him, 'that one of your performers is involved.'

'What!' Sanger exclaimed, smacking his desktop with such a blow that the inkbottle fairly jumped. 'Tell me how, by thunder! For if it's so, that person shall find himself promptly bundled off to Scotland Yard — and by God, by my own hand!'

Holmes explained briefly to the incensed circus master why he felt sure both acrobat and artist had been recruited to perpetuate the bizarre series of crimes. Yet he was extremely careful, I noted, not to mention Moriarty as the suspected organiser behind the scenes. (By then, of course, both Holmes and I had learned to guard ourselves, for while the professor was famous among criminals, his darker side was virtually unknown to the general public. Any mention of such a respected academic as a criminal, and I have no doubt we would have found ourselves hauled into court, and been ordered to pay a hefty solatium to assuage his wounded character.

'An acrobat, eh?' Sanger considered, after Holmes had finished. 'Well, gentlemen, we do have the best on the Continent. And, I'm not too modest to add, the best-paid lot as well. Shall we venture down to my back yard, then, and see if any have required more?'

Moments later the three of us were traversing the sawdust floor of the Amphitheatre's giant centre ring, where some members of the company were already performing the daily chore of rehearsing their various acts. That the towering balconies about us sat dark and empty mattered little; one could not step into that torch-lit ring without immediately being caught up in the colourful and exciting atmosphere the artists of the circus always seem to provide.

High above, a pair of aerialists spun gracefully in unison from one trapeze to the next, while before us a pretty young woman (whose costume, I felt, was decidedly daring) artfully juggled tenpins as she balanced on a wire. Next we came to a giant grey elephant, which bellowed frightfully as it reared up on command, lifting its huge front legs into the air. Following our host, we passed amidst tumblers and clowns, a dark-skinned contortionist, and a sword swallower who made me cringe as he calmly ingested the gleaming blade. As we approached the far side of the ring, Sanger called out to a tall, red-headed fellow who was standing near the entrance, motioning for him to join us.

'This is Archie Dennis, gentlemen,' Sanger informed us, as we met. 'If there's a better gaffer in England, I'm not aware. He keeps the Luck Boys out, the Tin

Plates happy, and he has his ear on every artist on my payroll.'

'Glad 'a meet yuh, guvs,' the tall man said. 'Is there sumthin' I kin do?'

'I require some information,' Sherlock Holmes replied. 'In particular, if you have an acrobat who has kept nocturnal hours of late.'

The tall man eyed my friend suspiciously, then tossed his employer a glance.

'Tell him what you know, Arch,' the circus master ordered. 'It could be nothing. Or, it could be business for the police.'

'Only one I know is Ulric. 'E's been leavin' after close; but not every night, mind yuh. Got a wench in Lambeth, so 'e says. 'Er 'usband's died, an' she's lookin' fer another.'

'How many times has he been to Lambeth in the last few weeks?'

'Three, maybe four, that I know of.'

'And this woman — have you seen her?'

'No. But 'e said 'er name was Sally.'

'I see.'

Holmes pointed toward a group of

athletic-looking gymnasts, four of whom were practising the Risley Act, some feet away. 'Which is Ulric?' he enquired.

'None of 'em, guv. Ulric ain't come out yet. I 'spect yuh'd find 'im in 'is wagon, back behind Clown Alley. If yuh'd like, I can show the way.'

'No need of that,' Sanger interposed. 'I'll look into this myself. Come along, gentlemen.'

We followed Sanger out of the ring and into the Amphitheatre's wide 'back yard', where the wagons and wardrobes containing the hundreds of properties used during each performance were stored. It was a busy place. All about us, workers were loading and unloading trunks and crates of various sizes, and moving tall, colourfully-painted back-drops to their respective and appointed places. Lions roared from their cages, a tethered line of horses was being fed, and the smell of coffee and spicy food was in the air. After passing between two rows of dressing rooms and tents, we finally came to a halt before a line of large, horse-drawn wagons, all brightly painted, the type of which all circus performers call home.

Sanger stepped up to the second of these, and pounded a harsh tattoo upon the door. 'Ulric!' he cried. 'Wake up, man! It's Sanger here, and I wish to speak with you!'

There was no answer, or sound from within. The curtained windows were dark. Again, Sanger knocked upon the door, and again there was no reply.

Anxiously, I glanced at Holmes, and felt my stomach tighten. His face was a grim mask. 'Something, I fear, has gone afoul,' he said. 'Lord George, that lamp, if you please.'

Holding the light before him, Holmes swung open the door and stepped up inside the acrobat's wagon. He had not gone far into its dark interior, before I heard his groan of abject dismay. 'We are too late,' he declared, as we joined him in a trice. 'Ulric is dead. He has been murdered.'

In the ruddy glow of the lamp, the body of the gymnast lay before us, sprawled grotesquely across the floor. He was lying on his back and was fully clothed, including his ulster, which hung open at the sides. Both his jacket and shirt beneath were heavily caked with blood.

'He appears to have been stabbed repeatedly,' I observed, kneeling down beside the corpse. 'And look here, Holmes! By that bruise across the temple, I'd say he was bludgeoned as well.'

'God help us all!' Sanger murmured. 'I shall send for the police immediately.'

'One moment!' Holmes insisted. 'We shall, I think, be better served by my looking round before the alarm is sounded. Strike more light, but I beg of you both, touch nothing!'

'What does this mean, Mr Holmes?' Sanger asked, as my companion was examining the body.

'It means there was no 'Sally'. It means that for the past two weeks, Ulric has been the man who so nimbly climbed atop the royal statues in the dead of night, with paint and brush in hand. For which, I'm sure, he was paid a handsome sum — one hundred pounds would be my guess.'

'He also paid with his life. You know who killed him, then?'

Holmes nodded. 'It was a confederate,' he answered. 'A hired assassin. A man whose speciality is the blade.'

He rose and strode to the small table on the far side of the chamber, where Sanger had struck another lamp. Beside it lay a bowler hat, a pair of gloves and a folded copy of the *Times*. My friend eyed them silently for a while, then knelt down and retrieved a charred matchstick from the floor.

'The sequence of events is easy to trace,' he stated. 'Ulric and the killer stepped inside the door, at which point Ulric — who was familiar with the room's interior — removed his hat and gloves, then struck a match and lit the lamp. That done, the killer knocked him senseless. After all, he could hardly risk the sounds of a struggle, or a cry for help, with others in such close proximity. And Ulric, while not a large man, was most certainly strong, and in excellent condition.'

'And then?'

'I have no doubt he dragged him thus,

clamped a hand to his mouth, and finished the deed.'

I shuddered. 'The mark of the professional,' I commented.

'Exactly. Lord George, you may call for the police.'

A crowd had begun to gather as we stepped down outside the wagon. After instructing the curious to keep their distance, Sanger set off to collar Archie Dennis and send him for the authorities, while we stood guard before the door of the dead man's trailer.

'Holmes,' I said, at length, being careful to lower my voice so no one else could hear, 'there is one point about all this I do wish you would explain.'

'And what is that?'

'Why on earth was Ulric killed? I mean, if your theory is correct, these Vandals must appear at least once more. If so, then who will paint the statue?'

My companion frowned. 'Who indeed? Perhaps there will be no more statues; my guess is that they've chosen another target instead. They discarded the ladder, after all. And now they have discarded the acrobat.' Try as he might, Holmes could not conceal the look of disappointment on his face. 'Things have taken a disturbing turn,' he admitted, dourly. 'Whatever Moriarty's scheme, I sense it is close to its climax. He is about to commit a truly heinous crime, Watson. And yet here we stand, baffled — I can almost hear him laughing.'

'So what will you do?'

'The only thing I can. I shall play my last card, and leave as soon as possible for Calais.'

* * *

An hour later, after conferring with Lestrade (at which time Holmes convinced both him and Sanger that the true facts behind Ulric's death must, for a time, be concealed), we hailed a cab and hurried back to our lodgings in Baker Street. No sooner was Holmes inside our door, than he quickly packed a bag and — after consulting his handy Bradshaw's — left for Victoria Station in order to catch the 12:35 express, which would put him in Dover by three. From there, Holmes said, he would board the first available steamer to Calais, where he would then seek out the art dealer, Claude Jarre. Naturally, I offered to accompany him, but Holmes refused. I was needed here, he told me, in case Potter or his sister happened to call, in the hope of securing riches. Should that happen, he said, I was to explain that the solicitor, Gardner (the surname he had given) was presently in Bristol on business, but would return by the afternoon train on Thursday. Might he meet them on that evening? And if so, what would be a convenient time, and where? Thus instructed, I was left to my ruminations.

The afternoon passed quickly enough. Holmes's absence finally allowed me a chance to devote my attention to Boothby's *A Brighton Tragedy*, a book I had hoped to get to for some time. A little after four, I put down my volume and lit the lamps, as the grey skies outside were darkening, then donned hat and coat and stepped out to purchase the evening papers, which I felt certain would carry accounts of Ulric's death. Lestrade and Sanger I found, had done their job well, for nowhere was any connection between the murdered acrobat and the Crimson Vandals mentioned. *Globe, News, Standard* and *Pall Mall Gazette* all carried lengthy stories on the 'Circus Murder' — but all were rather lurid accounts, hinting at a love affair gone wrong and a mysterious woman named Sally, whom the police were said to be seeking in connection with the case. Both Lestrade and Archie Dennis were quoted at length, while Sanger's name (no doubt, upon his instruction) was barely mentioned. Knowing Holmes would want to peruse the reports upon his return, I left them on his desk.

As was her habit, Mrs Hudson did her best to cheer me up at dinnertime, serving my favourite curry, juicy roast beef, and a crisp, light Yorkshire pudding, accompanied by a carafe of Burgundy. Upon conclusion of the meal, and braced by yet another glass of wine, I decided to try Holmes's methods, drawing my chair before the crackling fire with pipe in hand to cogitate a little on the facts of this most intriguing, yet puzzling, case. What, I wondered, could Moriarty possibly be up to? Clearly, the activities of the Crimson Vandals were a screen for some other plan, as yet not carried out. But what? A crime of immense importance, surely, else Holmes's life would not have been attempted. Had he been wrong for once? Was a member of the Royal House in danger? Based on all that had transpired thus far, I felt certain that some sort of destructive deed loomed before us. But where? Would we next find runic scrawls on the pillars of All Souls Church, or the cloistered entrance of the Inner Temple? Or (God help us?) splayed across the fountains at Buckingham Palace? Whatever the spot, I deduced that it must be close to home and within easy reach, as the services of the once-nimble Ulric were no longer required. And what of Potter, who had also sold his soul to the devil for one hundred pounds? By now, he must certainly know of the deaths of both Jacobsen and Ulric. If so, must he not fear for his own life as well? If only we could lay hands upon the man! And what had all this to do with Jacobsen, anyhow? What was the extent of his involvement with Moriarty? Holmes, I hoped, would be able to supply those answers upon his return from Calais. For the next few hours, my mind hashed and rehashed the facts as we now knew them, but the more I pondered (and refilled my glass) the less I was able to form any kind of concrete conclusion as to Moriarty's intent, or where he would strike next. This affair, I concluded, was certainly a convoluted one. As our mantel clock chimed ten, I considered filling another pipe and continuing with my book, but put the idea aside. The Burgundy, I found, had made me drowsy, and become warm and harsh upon my tongue. It was, I hoped, not a portent of things to come. As I dutifully extin- guished the lamps and stoked down the fire, I realised that my best course would be to secure a good night's sleep, be of stout heart, and pray for better on the morrow. Should Holmes require my assistance, I vowed, he would find me ready.

The following day, Holmes returned from Calais shortly after three in the afternoon, having caught (he said) an 11:45 special from Dover that allowed him to make Victoria Station by two. The sharp winter air, I noted, had brought a healthy flush to his normally pale complexion. But my heart sank at the look of disappointment on his face.

'You have learned nothing, then?' I ventured, prepared to accept the worst.

'On the contrary, Watson,' he replied, as he put down his bag and removed his coat and hat. 'I have learned much. But not enough, I fear.'

'Well, pray, tell me what you do know, at any rate. You have my full attention.'

Holmes moved before the fire, rubbing his hands together briskly. 'Monsieur Jarre, I found, was commissioned by Jacobsen to secure a painting, a canvas entitled 'Student at Leisure' by Paul Galpin. Which he did — it was, he said, for a Mr Cornelius.'

'Moriarty!'

'Connection number three, Watson. And here is number four: Galpin was an imitator of Jean Baptiste Greuze.'

'Greuze? — Hold on, I remember! Greuze is Moriarty's favourite painter! One of his works hangs over his desk.'[1] At that instant, something else about the name jangled in my brain, but for the life of me, I could not recall it.

'Jarre was told that the price was not an object,' Holmes continued, 'though a Galpin would hardly command a princely sum. There was one condition on the sale, however: if the painting was not delivered by the twentieth of this month, any offer was null and void.'

'The twentieth? Why, that was yesterday.'

'Precisely, Watson! It is that very fact which worries me most!'

Holmes began to drum his long fingers upon the mantel. It was, I knew, a sign of his deep frustration, and discontent.

'And why is that?' I asked.

'Because, obviously, such a condition

---

[1] *The Valley of Fear*, January 7–8, 1888.

suggests some sort of deadline. And that deadline has been met! It means, whatever Moriarty's scheme, that the final act may now occur at any time — perhaps even today!'

It was then, as Holmes reached despondently for his pipe and the Persian slipper, that his final word caused me to remember what had slipped my mind just moments before.

'Today,' I predicted smugly, 'Moriarty will have other things upon his mind. I suspect he will visit the National Gallery.'

'Oh?'

'Quite so, if he is the admirer of Greuze that you say. Two of his paintings have gone on display there. I read it in the *Times* this morning.'

Holmes's reaction to my words was hardly what I expected. For a long moment, he stared blankly past me, as if I were not even present. 'The National Gallery,' he murmured, finally.

'That is what I said,' I rejoined, reaching for the paper beside my chair. 'Here, read for yourself: *Head of a Girl* and *Boy with Lesson Book* are both on loan from the French.'

For another instant, my friend stood as if transfixed, though I could tell from the steely look in his eyes that his mind was racing feverishly. Clearly, my observation had struck a chord, although what I could not imagine. 'I have it, Watson!' he cried, suddenly, tossing aside his pipe and pouch. '*Boy with Lesson Book*! Don't you see? 'Truth, red says, is what is not'!'

'My dear Holmes, whatever do you mean?'

Holmes rushed across the room, and proceeded to throw on his coat and hat again. 'The cunning devil!' he exclaimed. 'He's going to steal a Greuze — and no one will ever suspect!'

'Where are we off to, then?' I asked, as I hurried for my things as well. 'Scotland Yard, I presume?'

'There is no time to inform Lestrade,' my friend replied. 'Fate has left this in our hands alone. Arm yourself, Watson — but hurry. We must make Trafalgar Square at once! The doors of the gallery close at dusk!'

Moments later we were bouncing along

in a hailed conveyance through the snowy streets of London. Holmes had promised our cabbie an extra guinea if we made Trafalgar Square by four o'clock, and the fellow was doing his best with whip and reins to earn it, despite the heavy traffic.

'As usual, you are a step ahead of me, Holmes,' I confessed, hanging on for dear life as our vehicle lurched wildly round a corner, drawing angry cries from the startled pedestrians whom we had just narrowly missed. 'However, then, did you deduce that Moriarty plans to steal a Greuze?'

'From the rhyme, Watson. And that gem of knowledge which you so off-handedly provided.'

'You mean, that the paintings were on display?'

'Yes. When you mentioned the National Gallery, and the thought of Moriarty being there, it was as if a shaft of light had cut through the darkness! The outline of his malevolent scheme suddenly became clear. He orders a Galpin — a fake Greuze, if you will — which must be delivered by the twentieth. The following

day, the real thing goes on display. And!
— in a place where the Crimson Vandals
would need no acrobat or ladder in order
to strike. The conclusion was inescapable:
Moriarty would substitute the cheap
Galpin for the valuable Greuze, leaving
no one else the wiser.'

'But, Holmes, that is impossible! Any
art critic worth his salt would immediately know the difference.'

'Not after the Crimson Vandals had
done their work. Remember the line,
Watson! 'Truth, red says, is what is not.'
That was the Vandals' final task — to
make it appear that both Greuzes had
been destroyed. When, in actuality, one
was a cheap Galpin.'

'But why go to all the trouble to
purchase a Galpin? It would seem to me
that any painting of the same approximate
size would do as well.'

'Hardly, Watson. Moriarty is well aware
that the charred remains would come
under close examination. The surviving
pieces of canvas and frame must have the
proper age. I also suspect he plans to
leave behind a fragment or two, in which

the colouring is similar. Oh, yes! — He has thought this all out quite thoroughly.'

'How diabolical! I cannot imagine any person so evil as to conceive of such a plan.'

'The evil of man is as inventive as it is immeasurable, Watson. That is what makes Moriarty so unique. He has turned wickedness into a science.'

'I must ask again, Holmes: would we not be far better off to alert the police?'

'What, and sound the alarm? No, no. Moriarty, I'm sure, has taken pains to place one or two confederates inside the building. The sudden sight of uniforms would only cause them all to fly.'

'Still — '

Holmes motioned me to silence. 'It is, I realise, an enormous risk we take,' he admitted, 'but think of the reward: Should we catch the professor in the act, we shall finally place him in the dock.'

'He won't be there in person, surely?'

My companion gave me a knowing look. 'With something so close to his evil heart at stake,' he stated, firmly, 'I cannot believe he would stay away.'

At precisely one minute to four, our cab rolled to a halt before the broad façade of the National Gallery, not ten yards from the spot where we had alighted with Lestrade two days before. How much had happened, I mused, since then. Stepping into the street, we were immediately dwarfed by the towering row of Corinthian columns and the large black tympanum which marked the main entrance to the building, facing Trafalgar Square. The grey winter sky, I noted, with a chill, had already begun to darken. A few snowflakes laced the air, and a cold wind whipped angrily at my cheeks.

After settling with our driver (including the promised guinea), we climbed the three wide flights of concrete stairs leading to the Gallery's huge front portico, where we paused a moment to catch our breath, then hurried on inside. To my surprise, large numbers of people were milling about the ornately-decorated vestibules, which lined the outer hall and opened into the various wings of the museum; more so, I knew, than was usual for that hour. Tours, I observed, were also still under way. I could only conclude that the arrival of the two French masterpieces had sparked a considerable interest among the art-lovers and patrons of the city. Including, I thought grimly, one particularly demented academic, whom Holmes and I had somehow to thwart at any cost.

'Well, Holmes,' I asked, as my friend paused before the directory, 'what is our plan?'

'We shall first locate the Greuze display, and then view the works in that vicinity,' he replied. 'We must appear as inconspicuous as possible, while I search for a place to hide.'

'Hide?'

'But of course, Watson. How else to surprise Moriarty, save from a nearby place of concealment? We can hardly wait for him in the lobby, hat in hand — Ah, here we are! The French School, Room twenty-eight. In the West Wing. Come along.'

In a trice we had whisked our way out of the West Vestibule, and then continued on through two rooms of the British

School, which along with the French, Parmesan, Bolognese and Spanish, occupied the entire West Wing of the building. The first, I glimpsed as we hurried along, was devoted mainly to Hogarth, including his famous *Marriage à la mode*, and the second featured early English landscapes by Scott, Gainsborough, Crome and others. Turning to our right, we soon found ourselves at the entrance to Room twenty-eight, on whose walls, I observed, hung works of French Primitives such as Marmion and de Lyon; my attention was immediately drawn to Carmontelle's fine watercolour of Mozart as a child, but before I could linger, Holmes gently tugged the sleeve of my coat and urged me on.

In the far corner of the room, an elegant dark green drapery had been hung, and before it, displayed on handsome easels of polished red mahogany, were the two borrowed portraits by Jean Baptiste Greuze. Silently, we took our places behind a dozen or so people who stood before the canvasses in rapt attention, listening to a dissertation on the painter and his works being given by a uniformed guide.

'We have cut this decidedly close,' Holmes whispered, glancing at the skylights above. 'The light is fading fast. I doubt they will remain open another quarter-hour. Wait here, while I have a quick look about.'

Thus left to my own devices, I first made an examination of the visitors before me, on the chance that Moriarty — or perhaps a suspicious-looking cohort — might be among them. They were not. Finding the guide's perfunctory monotone uninteresting, I decided to focus my complete attention upon the two paintings themselves, and apply what meagre appreciation I possessed until Holmes returned. *Head of a Girl*, whose languishing face was framed in soft brown hair, was, I decided, too melancholy for my taste. *Boy with Lesson Book*, however, was quite another matter. In the soft, radiant face of the student, I felt, Greuze had admirably captured both the innocence and enquiring mind of youth; the boy's brooding, meditative eyes seemed to be trying to fathom the mysteries of life itself, rather than the mere problem posed from the open lesson book before him. The sensitivity of his features, however — especially his delicate hands — I found disturbing, as they seemed to hint at weakness, as well as virtue. Was this, I wondered, why Moriarty desired the painting so? Because, on one hand, it harkened back to his own youthful thirst for knowledge, when he was regarded as one of the most brilliant theologians in the land? And, because it also seemed to confirm his own later-acquired belief that virtue was, when tested, a weakness — and that pure, logical, evil was, in reality, the only true strength? I shuddered at the thought, and reverently hoped that within the next few hours, come what may, I would possess my father's good Scot's strength.

My reverie was suddenly broken by a tap upon my shoulder. I turned to see my friend.

'The Bolognese exhibit demands our

attention, Watson,' he declared, just loud enough to cause a few heads to turn. 'Come, come. Dolci's *Madonna* awaits.'

No sooner had we removed ourselves to the adjoining room, than Holmes quickly pulled me aside. 'Our choices, as I feared, are few,' he said, speaking low. 'I had hoped we might repair to the small closet across the room. Alas, it is locked. And, as I'm sure you will agree, the curtains at either entrance could hardly conceal us both.'

'So what, then?'

'We are fortunate the paintings have been exhibited in such a manner,' Holmes replied. 'We shall position ourselves behind the display.'

'But is there sufficient cover?' I asked, somewhat taken aback.

'Enough, I'd say. I was able to glimpse some packing crates, as I walked past, which have been stored behind the curtain. If you are not averse to using the floor, Doctor, I think they will do nicely. Ah, good! The group is moving on. Come along. Once they've gone, we shall take up our positions.'

Re-entering the French room, we stationed ourselves before the two Gruezes, behaving as if we were viewing the paintings. The last of the tour group, I noted from the corner of my eye, was leaving at the other side. For a long moment, we stood alone in that large, silent chamber, in which the light was now rapidly fading.

Holmes glanced warily about. 'Upon my signal, Watson,' he hissed, 'step behind the curtain. I shall follow, as is convenient.'

The floor, I found some seconds later, was hard indeed, and our quarters exceedingly cramped. Encumbered by my heavy outer coat, it was all I could do to kneel down clumsily behind the crates and lean my back against the wall, thankful for its firm support. A moment later, Holmes joined me in that small space and followed suit.

'From now on, not a sound,' he warned, his voice a whisper. 'And not a move, unless I say. Remember, we must give them time to do their work before we spring.'

Thus, our wait began.

It was, I could not help but recall, our second such nocturnal vigil in two months, the first having been in the infamous D'Arcy affair (chronicled earlier in this volume), which involved the schemings of Moriarty as well. On that night, matters had been brought to a successful conclusion; I could only hope that once again such would be the case. What troubled me, however, as I waited beside Holmes in the darkening room, was the knowledge that on this occasion, we were not accompanied by the police.

A short time later, we heard a single set of footsteps approaching, their soft click-clack accompanied by the roving, yellow beam of a bulls-eye lantern. As the steps paused before the curtain, and the light was flashed about, Holmes and I exchanged a nervous glance. It was only when the light had gone away, and the footsteps were receding, that we dared breathe a sigh of relief. The gallery, it was clear, had closed; the guards had begun their evening rounds.

Another half-hour and we were in total

darkness. Owing to the constant strain of kneeling, my legs were aching to the point where I felt I must, if only slightly, shift my weight. As I started to move, however, I felt Holmes's steady grip upon my arm. It was then that I heard it, too: the sound of footsteps again, coming rapidly our way. And then, the low, unmistakable murmur of voices! Forgetting the pain, I withdrew my revolver and focused all my attentions outward. By the sounds, it was clear, that at least three people were approaching. Would Moriarty, I wondered, be among them?

Seconds later, my question was chillingly answered, when the footsteps ceased and lantern light glowed from the other side of the curtain. I heard faint, scraping noises, as if objects were being moved, or placed upon the floor.

'There will, I presume, be no interruptions?' My blood ran cold; it was the same soft, yet terrifying voice I had first heard in Baker Street some weeks ago, and which, I knew, belonged to only one man.

'No, Professor. Every watchman in this

wing has his copper — or a threat that's worth as much.'

Moriarty uttered an evil chuckle. 'Good. I must confess, Langdon, you seem a talented man. I was told you were a mere assassin, a knifeman and garrotter. Your abilities, however, seem to have been vastly underrated. I shall not forget.'

'Thank you, Professor.'

'The carriage waits outside?'

'It does. And with a driver who's papered well. Should any peeler[1] enquire, he's on an errand for Burton[2] himself this night.'

'My, my! You have done well. I can see that we were quite fortunate in placing you here, even on short notice. I do not exaggerate when I say that your efforts have eased our task considerably.'

'And the painting, Professor? Shall I place it in the coach?'

'No, not yet. If discovered, it could

---

[1] A policeman.

[2] Fredrick William Burton, director of the National Gallery.

prove difficult to explain — besides, I wish to study it a bit, while Potter concludes his work. Savour the moment, you might say, although I doubt you understand my meaning.'

'That's not my business,' the other quickly replied. 'The whys don't interest me much. I just carry out my orders, as I'm told.'

'A laudable attitude, I assure you. Maintain it, and you will go far in my organisation. Suffice to say, some months ago in Durham, I was deprived of my proper position in academia. Just like that! And all because, I felt, of what amounted to a petty misdemeanour. It was an aberration, given my standing, which should have been allowed.'

'Ah, you've been settling accounts, then?'

'Yes, in a fashion.' Moriarty's words were coldly measured now, laced with a bitterness heavy as lead. 'In my own manner, I have secured revenge. The fool who betrayed me is dead. The institute which denied me has suffered. And now, I possess a student of my own. *The* prize student, you understand? It is, I feel, a definite tribute. A trophy, if you will, to my superior intellect. It is a class of one — which no academic wretch can take away!'

For a moment, there was an awkward silence. Although the heavy curtain blocked our view, I sensed that Moriarty was struggling to compose himself, his malevolent anger spent.

'Potter,' he enquired, finally, his voice again its deadly calm, 'how long until you are finished?'

'N-not long, Professor,' assured a third voice, which I took to be that of the artist. 'The message is down. I need only to splatter the easels and the floor — and the Galpin, once the change has been made.'

'Well, do it then. But, mind you! Take great care not to damage the other Greuze. Who knows? It, too, may be mine one day. Langdon, fetch the lamp oil and matches from the bag.'

It was at that moment Holmes sprang to his feet, pistol in hand, and stepped out from behind the curtain. 'Stand fast, all of you!' he ordered, as I quickly made his side. 'Well, well. Professor Moriarty. Or should I say, Mr Cornelius? Your ruse of the Crimson Vandals has been most entertaining.'

Moriarty allowed us a sour smile. I shuddered. Pure hatred showed in his black eyes. 'I did not expect you would be present, sir,' he replied, with an evil sneer, 'or I assure you I would have made my little charade more challenging.'

Beside him, holding a small burlap sack, stood the killer Langdon, dangerous-looking and strongly built. A step behind cowered Potter, red-tipped brush in hand, a small, thin fellow with a frightened look upon his face. *Head of a Girl*, I noted, had been reversed, and a line of runic figures painted across the paper backing of the frame. *Boy with Lesson Book* appeared untouched, and a third canvas, which I assumed was the Galpin, leaned against its easel.

'I am complimented that you took such pains in trying to dispatch me,' Holmes rejoined. 'It makes this moment that much more rewarding. This time, my dear Professor, you shall not escape the justice you deserve. — Disarm them, Watson. But carefully!'

Once behind them, I removed a considerable haul, relieving Moriarty of his revolver and stick, Langdon of a pistol and a knife tucked inside his boot, and Potter of a small derringer, which was strapped to his arm beneath his sleeve.

'Now,' Holmes said, picking up a lantern, 'if you will permit me — '

Motioning the others back, he then stepped forward and held the light above the line of the crimson markings, while I kept watch, knowing full well the fatal danger that lurked beyond the barrel of my weapon.

'Let me see,' Holmes murmured, 'how does it go?

'Red conceals the circle
'As trees conceal the land.
'Red conceals all knowledge
'Behind which real truth stands.
'Truth, red says, is what is not — ''

He paused a moment to scan the line.

''And what's not is in my hands.'

'My congratulations, Professor! You could not, I trust, have written a better confession. For you and Potter, it means a prison term — and the death sentence for 'Bloody Jack'.'

At that instant, I started, as something cold and hard touched the back of my neck!

'That may well be,' a voice behind me said, 'but only after this gentleman's brains are blown to kingdom come! Your choice, Mr Sherlock Holmes! You have five seconds to decide!'

'Holmes!' I cried. 'Don't — '

My protestation was cut short by Holmes's almost imperceptible gesture of resignation, as he dropped his revolver to the floor. I was then quickly relieved of mine as well.

'I knew you were out there somewhere, Sanders,' Moriarty remarked, as he and the others rearmed themselves. 'Your timing, however, was exquisite. Oh yes, it really was.'

As the fourth man stepped round into the light, I could not conceal my amazement. It was none other than the fake policeman, who had burst into our rooms, then vanished, four days ago in Baker Street!

'No need for any Hindu mumbo-jumbo this time 'round,' he chortled. 'These fish are ready to fry.'

A sickening feeling welled up inside me. My worst fears had come to pass. We were in Moriarty's clutches; our fate was in his hands.

'How ironic that we spoke of settling accounts,' Moriarty mused, as Potter began splattering paint about. 'Let me see. Rope and another carriage are what we need.'

'There's rope in the closet below the stairs,' Langdon said, knowingly. He snapped his fingers. 'And I can call a cab just that quick.'

The ogre smiled. 'Good. They shall go with us, then — once our work here is done.'

Moments later, our wrists were tightly bound. A cry for help, we both knew, would be of little use, given Langdon's earlier preparations. Helplessly, Holmes and I watched as he doused the Galpin and its stand with kerosene, then drenched both the carpet and the curtain with the smelly fluid as well. A small holocaust, I could see, was in the making.

For a time Moriarty, too, had watched this all in silence, arms crossed, his chin resting thoughtfully in his hand. Then, as if emerging from a dream, he suddenly uttered an exclamation, a look of immense satisfaction upon the deepset lines of his drawn, pasty-white face. Moving quickly to my companion's side, he raised his sleeve, and removed one of the silver links which held his shirtcuffs in place.

'It is my understanding,' Holmes told him, 'that cannibals only strip the dead.'

'Believe me,' Moriarty said, his fangs bared in a frozen smile, 'I shall try my utmost to accommodate you. Oh yes, I really shall! Let us just call this a souvenir of the occasion.'

The monster swung round, riveting us both in his evil gaze. 'I feel I must warn you both,' he said, in his soft, precise way, 'that once we reach the door, your lives are in each other's hands. A cry from either of you in the street, and Langdon will do for the other — ' He made a short, stabbing motion with his hand. ' — Silently, and quickly.'

'All's ready, Professor,' the massive killer said.

Taking the box of matches, Moriarty struck one, and tossed it in the direction of the painting. With a blinding flash, the fire ignited the oil, and flames shot up before us! The Galpin and its ornate wooden stand were immediately engulfed, as more licks of fire crept quickly toward the curtain — which suddenly exploded into a white-hot sheet of flame, scorching the air so fiercely that we all were forced to back away!

The horror of that dreadful moment will remain forever etched in my mind. The heat, the smoke, the burning smell, the terrifying yellow glare of the consuming blaze — in whose awful glow, I saw a look of hideous pleasure on Moriarty's wicked face.

As we were hurried along down the darkened corridor, alarm bells began to sound. Macabre light from the flames behind us danced upon the walls. Not unlike a funeral pyre, I thought, or what must welcome a soul to hell.

★ ★ ★

Langdon, unfortunately, was as good as his word, and we were quickly off — Moriarty, the Greuze and Sanders occupying the first cab; Langdon, Holmes and myself in the second. Snow was falling heavily again, and it softened the clip-clops of our horse's hooves, as we moved off down the street. The assassin said nothing, merely eyeing us carefully, a revolver in his left hand, a gleaming stiletto in the right. As the blue, sputtering arc lamps passed by outside, I repeatedly wondered if either Holmes or myself should not try to make some break, but a look at my companion told me that this was not the moment. We must bide our time, and hope for a better opportunity.

As to our destination, I could only guess. We seemed to be heading in the general direction of the river. My suspicions were soon confirmed, when we came upon the orange-lit windows and iron gates of Charing Cross Hotel and Station. How many times, I recalled as we rattled past, had Holmes and I set out from there on some wild and mysterious adventure? The grisly death of Sir Eustace Brackenstall,[1] and our curious trip to Yoxley Old Place,[2] immediately sprang to mind.

Turning left onto the Embankment,[3] which bordered the dark waters of the Thames, our coach continued on a little way before slowing to a halt. At Langdon's signal, we stepped out into the

---

[1] *The Adventure of the Abbey Grange*, January 23, 1897.

[2] *The Adventure of the Golden Pince-Nez*, November 14–15, 1894.

[3] The Victoria Embankment, an impressive boulevard constructed in 1864–70, upon the left bank of the Thames. Cleopatra's Needle was put there in 1878.

swirling snow, only to find ourselves standing at the base of Cleopatra's Needle, the sixty-foot granite obelisk originally cut from the quarries of the Aswan, which now marked a concrete mooring located along the Embankment's edge.

Looking north, the lights of the city blinked and gleamed in the wintry night. Waterloo Bridge, I knew, loomed somewhere in the darkness, and beyond it, Doctors' Commons. At our captors' urging, we descended the steps which led to the water's edge. A motor launch was waiting.

No sooner had we stepped on board than the captain swung away, smoke belching from his vessel's single stack, and we set off down the darkened Thames, with the wind and the flakes of snow it bore whipping at our faces. My initial thought was to turn up the collar of my greatcoat, but my bound hands would not allow it. As we moved further away from shore, Langdon ordered Holmes and me to seat ourselves at the rear of the boat, then joined the others, who were standing next to the low bulkhead of the cabin, some feet away. Moriarty, I noted, did not seem to mind that his lieutenant had relaxed his watch; after all, our hands were securely tied, and save for the icy waters all round, where else for us to go?

'I could stick 'em here, and dump 'em easy, Professor,' the burly killer suggested. 'A bit of ballast, and nobody but the fish would ever see the bodies.'

Moriarty's evil reply was even more chilling than the gusts of wind and snow which stung at my cheeks and throat. 'No doubt you are right,' he agreed, placing a complimentary hand to the other's shoulder. 'As to means, it would certainly be most efficient. However, it seems to me, well — so uninspired. I have something more imaginative in mind.'

A sense of both anger and fear welled up inside me. What now, I thought, what now?

'Holmes, we must do something,' I whispered, as we passed beneath Blackfriars Bridge, leaving the glowing streetlamps of the Embankment behind. 'Good Lord, I feel like a sheep being led to the slaughter.'

'What would you have us do, Watson?' he rejoined. 'Weapons and freedom of movement would most certainly improve our odds, but at the moment, we have neither. However, I think our chance may come when we reach shore.'

'Ah,' I said, 'you have a plan, then?'

'Not a very original one, I'm afraid. But somehow one of us must break free — to summon help, and quickly.'

'You then, surely. You are much quicker afoot than I, and thus more able to avoid pursuit.'

My companion smiled. 'Watson, I swear,' he said, 'you are living proof that a stubborn heart shall best evil at the last! I can only pray this works — else we are hard against it.'

As best I could estimate, another half-hour passed by before our craft — which had kept studiously to the middle of the channel — finally veered to the left and swung back towards the shore. The biting wind had left my face frozen, and my limbs were stiff, as we had been unable to move about. One thing, however, was clear: we had ventured well downstream to the far East End, for we had long ago passed through the Tower Bridge construction, and since left behind the docks of the Thames Police at Wapping, and the Shadwell Basin as well. If my calculations were correct, we were presently chugging south by east, somewhere off the Isle of Dogs.

It hit me then, as we began to close on the blinking lights that marked the approaching shoreline: we were being taken to Moriarty's Lair, hidden in the West India Docks near Limehouse! That he would take such a risk, I knew, could mean only that he did not plan that either of us should survive.

Leaving the main channel, we slowed, and began to make our way through the seemingly endless wharves, past row after row of barges, launches and other small craft, all tied up for the night. Here and there in the snowy darkness the gleam of a lamp could be seen, from the window of a fisherman's shanty. Off to our right, a dog began barking furiously, then just as suddenly, was quiet. On we went. Save for the soft chug of our engine, and the churning of the water beneath us, I could hear no other sound. Glancing at Holmes, I discerned a look of quiet resolution on his face. The end of our journey, we both knew, was not far off. Our fate, at best, appeared uncertain. But we had made plans, and we were ready.

A short time later, our launch nudged gently to a halt against the side of a snow-covered dock, whose weathered posts and creaking boards were all but hidden in the shadow of an ageing warehouse, built nearly a century before at the river's edge. The place, clearly, was in a state of some decay; its dark windows were cracked and boarded, the grimy brickwork scarred and worn. In spite of the freshness of the cold, the dank, foul smells of the river quickly rose up to meet us, the taint of fish and waste and rotting wood, all heavy on the senses. Adjoining the grim-looking structure was a continuing flight of wooden stairs which led to the street above, where the yellow glow of a lone street lamp showed resolutely through the falling snow.

It was upon that staircase and that lamp (which seemed to me, a beacon of hope) that Holmes directly affixed his gaze, before giving me a confirming nod.

As he had expected, it was Moriarty who stepped off first, hurrying along with Sanders to the rear door of the warehouse, clutching close his treasured prize. Langdon was next, levelling his pistol in Holmes's direction, as he raised a foot and followed.

It was then, in that fraction of a second it took for me to put my foot upon the rail, that Holmes quickly stepped to the killer's other side, causing him to momentarily look away.

With all my strength, I propelled myself up and forward, smashing into Langdon! His gun went off, firing harmlessly into the air, and Holmes was off like a sprinter out of the block — making for the staircase as we both fell to the boards. As best I could, I threw my full weight upon the man, hoping to gain my friend those precious seconds I knew he needed, if he was to make it safely out of range.

Cursing heartily, Langdon threw me off, and raised his arm to fire. Again, I heaved into him, and again his shot went astray — the bullet throwing off sparks as it struck and ricocheted off the dingy brick, not a foot from Holmes's side!

Struggling to my knees, I heard Moriarty's scream of rage, as Holmes continued on. Then something struck me from behind; my senses blurred, and I slipped to the ground again. The last thing I remembered, before the dark closed in, was how hard the ancient planking felt, and cold snowflakes on my cheek . . .

★ ★ ★

When I woke, my head ached mightily, and my ears were soundly ringing. My first impression, as my vision cleared, was of the ropes above me, which now not only bound my wrists, but held me captive in a chair. Before me was a desk and upon it an oil lamp burning bright. On the other side, Moriarty and Langdon stood, gazing down intently in my direction. The professor, I vaguely realised, was speaking.

' — as Dr Watson, I see, has finally regained his consciousness. How very excellent. Our party is again complete.'

Complete? The word jangled alarmingly at my senses! Glancing about, I recognised Sanders standing some feet away — and beside him Holmes, his hands still bound!

I tried to sort things out. What could have happened? Surely, Holmes had made the street . . .

'This was, I'm sure, not the result you have intended,' Moriarty remarked, noting my puzzled gaze. 'Still, I do commend you both on such audacity. It almost worked, you know. Oh my, it nearly did! Had two of my lurkers[1] not heard the shots I seriously doubt that Mr Holmes would have been waylaid.'

'And what of you, Watson?' Holmes enquired. 'Are you seriously injured?'

'No,' I replied, 'I was struck from

---

[1] Criminals used as lookouts, or to follow others, oft-times in disguise. Also known as crows.

behind but I am beginning to come round.'

'Ah, Langdon's work, no doubt,' Holmes said, the words dripping with distaste. 'It is, I imagine, the full extent of his expertise.'

The huge killer snarled angrily, drawing out his knife, but Holmes ignored him, stepping forward to lock his steely gaze upon the peering black eyes of our evil captor. 'I am not a man to beg,' he stated, fiercely, 'but I must ask that you release my friend. You know, as well as I, that he is no danger to you. Do that — then deal as you will with me.'

As I tried to object, Moriarty motioned me to silence, then slowly shook his large, domed head with what I took to be an expression of finality. 'It is a laudable gesture, sir,' he admitted, a waxen smile upon his craggy face. 'Truly, I am affected. But no, I really cannot do it. You see, it would spoil my little plan.'

'And what is that?' Holmes asked.

The professor chuckled. 'Why, to create a mystery, Mr Holmes! The final mystery of your career! Oh, it will be a tangled skein, I do assure you. So tangled and full of contradiction that the truth will never be discovered. A century from now, I daresay, it shall be this night you are remembered for, as much as your previous successes.'

'The cufflink,' Holmes stated.

'Ah! — The power of your intellect never fails to disappoint me. Or was it merely that you saw me place it?'

'Hardly. The connection is a rather simple one to make.'

'Make it, then.'

'My cufflink is found at the scene of the crime. We are found here, with Potter's brush and paint. That I recently sought knowledge of runes could easily be attested to. We were seen entering the gallery at dusk, but did not leave. Circumstantial evidence, to be sure. But evidence, none the less.'

My heart sank. Before me again passed the askew glances of the tour group. And what cabbie would forget a guinea tip?

'My blushes, sir!' Moriarty exclaimed. 'Why, it seems you are on to me entirely. However, there are a few embellishments

I have yet in mind. Your jewellery was but the first strand of the web — ' He gave Sanders an urgent nod. 'Bring him in.'

A moment later, the artist stood before us.

'You have done well,' Moriarty told him, 'unlike that wretched acrobat, who attempted to raise his price. Fortunately, his services were no longer needed.'

From the pocket of his coat, the professor drew an envelope, which he then handed to the man. 'A bonus,' he said, with the slightest smile. 'Your ticket and expenses. The Costa del Sol is marvellous at this time of year.' The sinister tone of Moriarty's voice left no doubt that the other would not refuse. 'If you return before I send for you,' he added, 'I shall find it very inappropriate. Do you understand?'

'I-I do, Professor.'

'Good. — Oh, before you go, I have a final request. A simple task, I assure you, which will only take a moment. Just sprinkle some paint across this gentleman's trousers, will you? And put the slightest smudge upon his shoe.'

'Another strand?' Holmes observed, sarcastically.

Moriarty's look turned cold. 'The first of many I have in store,' he replied, while the painter did as he was told. 'Thank you, Potter. Sanders has a coach outside. He will see you to your ship.'

'Y-yes, sir. Goodbye, Professor.'

'Now, where was I?' Moriarty mused, after they had gone. 'Oh, yes — we were talking of embellishments.'

He picked up both our weapons, which had been lying upon the desk, then weighed them carefully for a moment, one in either hand. 'Now, how shall this be done?' he asked himself. 'Shall I first train Dr Watson's gun on you, then yours on him? Or shall I let one pistol do the work? — Why, of course! That's it. Why, Fleet Street will have a field day! I can see the tabloids now: 'Murder — Suicide! The Strange Death of Sherlock Holmes!'

'And what of motive, you say? Why, what better than a hint of megalomania? After all, your disdain of the official force is commonly known. How better then to prove your point, than to play them such a game, while you investigate yourself? Tut, tut. And to think that I, a simple man of letters, was to be the scapegoat for your dementia? For shame, sir. For shame. Of course, we shall need a note in Dr Watson's hand, which will surface later, alluding to your condition. What shall we say led to his downfall, Doctor? Morphine? Or cocaine?'

'You fiend!' I cried. 'You'll get nothing of the sort from me! My hand shall wither, before it writes such a line!'

'Come, come, Doctor,' the monster replied, a gleam of perverse pleasure in his eye. 'There is more than one hypnotist in Limehouse, after all. I imagine we could secure another within an hour — ' Hypnotist? The word jangled something in my brain. ' — Or would you rather we fetched your dear landlady, Mrs Hudson, and brought her here to plead our case?'

'You wouldn't dare!' I shouted, straining at the ropes which bound me. 'Surely, you are not so despicable! May the devil take you, sir! — If you are not the devil, himself.'

'Calm yourself, Watson,' Holmes interjected. 'He is enjoying this, can't you see? Moriarty, do your worst, I say! But spare us your pitiable madness.'

Angry colour rushed to the professor's pale cheeks, and his head began to oscillate slowly from side to side. For a moment, I thought his condition to be apoplectic. 'Madness, you call it!' he stormed. 'I call it power, Mr Holmes! Power which forces others to do my bidding! Oh, you may scoff, sir, but it is so. Far more than you realise. The police may patrol the streets, but on the East End the power of life and death is mine!'

Moriarty lay Holmes's pistol down upon the desk. Again, I strained with all my might, but the ropes remained secure. Was there nothing I could do?

'I know a hundred men who would pay dearly for this moment,' Moriarty declared, as he turned again to face my friend. 'But in this case, I shall forgo profit for some pleasure. It shall be I who plays the final trick.'

Pausing, he produced a scrap of paper, which he held triumphantly before him. 'I nearly forgot,' he said. 'This is the final garnish. The receipt for the Galpin. I shall place it in your pocket, sir, after you are gone. Watch carefully, then, Dr Watson! I shall now succeed, where you once failed! How does it feel, Mr Sherlock Holmes, to fall victim to your own trap?'

Trap! Trap! It struck me, then! The words of Porlock's message! A trap door, hidden before Moriarty's desk — where he was standing now! But how to trigger it? There must, I knew, be a latch of some sort close by. With all my strength, I edged down in the chair, and began to frantically search, with my feet, beneath the desk.

Moriarty raised his arm to fire.

'These will be your last ten seconds on earth, Mr Holmes,' he said, as he levelled the barrel at my companion's chest. 'When you are gone, I must admit, it will be a considerable relief. Ten, nine — '

Wildly, I moved my legs and feet about, feeling nothing but the smoothness of the wood.

'Eight, seven, six — '

Right side, nothing! Left side, nothing!

In desperation, I raised my knees, first right, then left, running them as quickly as I dared along the underside of the middle drawer. I froze! Langdon had turned his gaze my way! My heart was pounding! It seemed an eternity until he looked away again, anxious to view my friend's demise . . .

'Four, three — '

What if the switch was inside a drawer? The thought was too awful to contemplate.

'Two, one.'

There it was! My left knee had brushed against what felt like the edge of a metal button, not an inch from the front of the drawer! With all my strength, I pushed my leg up against it, then let forth a blood-curdling yell — which gained me a precious second or two, as Moriarty and Langdon whirled round!

For a heartbeat, all I could hear was the crash of boards, and Moriarty's terrified scream, as he dropped from my view! Seeing my revolver clatter across the floor, I surged to my feet, carrying the wooden chair behind me. Quick as a cat,

Langdon drew his knife, then staggered — Moriarty, I saw, was hanging from his leg!

It was at that instant that Holmes lunged forward, positioned himself, and sent a devastating kick into the big man's side. Dropping his weapon, Langdon groaned, then sank to one knee at the edge of the black abyss.

I did not hesitate. With a well-placed shove, I sent both him and the evil professor plummeting into the darkness! For the briefest of seconds, we heard their cries, a splash — then nothing more.

Grabbing Langdon's knife, Holmes quickly cut loose my ropes, after which I did the same for him. I could tell, as we stood there, looking into each other's eyes, that he was greatly moved.

'God bless you, Watson,' he said, finally. 'What was that you said about a faithful friend being a strong defence? They are words, I promise you, I shall not forget.'

'What do we do now, then?' I enquired, as we hastened to retrieve our weapons.

'We shall make the street, and hail a cab!' Holmes answered. 'As to the professor's minions, do not hesitate! Shoot any who might try to interfere!'

Uttering a sigh, my friend reached for the singular canvas that had been the cause of so much recent destruction, agony and suffering. 'And this, of course,' he said, 'goes with us. For the night, it should be safe enough at Baker Street.'

Glancing back at the empty black hole, I felt a surge of relief flood through my veins, and a heartfelt sense of vindication as well. Moriarty had used me as a tool to try and kill my friend; at least, now, I had done for him instead.

'How many poor souls have gone before him?' I pondered, half-aloud. 'This was, it seems to me, a fitting place for so evil a man to meet his end.'

'Yes, if it indeed proves so,' Holmes agreed. 'One wonders if you can ever kill the devil, Watson. But, come along. We still have much to do this night.'

If Moriarty's guards were still on watch, the gleam of our revolvers must have kept them in the shadows. At any rate, we were not molested. Two blocks away, we secured a conveyance, and returned without incident through the softly-falling snow to the welcome warmth and security of our tried and familiar lodgings.

★ ★ ★

The following morning, I awoke shortly after six, dressed quickly, and rushed hurriedly through my toilet. Holmes had despatched telegrams to both Lestrade and his brother, Mycroft, upon our return the night before, asking that they call on us at Baker Street at seven o'clock. It was a conversation, quite naturally, that I did not want to miss.

My timing, I discovered, could hardly have been better. As I entered our cosy sitting room, Mrs Hudson was just leaving, having placed upon our table a steaming pot of coffee and a hearty supply of toast and jam, to which Mycroft was busily applying his attentions. Lestrade, I could see, had only just arrived, as he was removing his hat and heavy topcoat, both of which were lightly flecked with snow. Beside the plates, I glimpsed a copy of the morning *Times*, and a headline which immediately caught my eye:

PAINTING LOST!
National Gallery
Damaged by Fire

'Ah, Watson!' Holmes enthused, as I shook our visitors' hands. 'You have your notebook, I see. Excellent! What better than my faithful Boswell, present to record the finish? Pour yourself some coffee, won't you? I was about to relate to these good gentlemen the story of our travails, as well as the telling facts in this lurid case!'

Upon hearing the words, Lestrade appeared to be taken aback. He cast the detective a doubting glance. 'No disrespect, Mr Holmes,' he stated, with what I took to be some satisfaction, 'but I think you should be aware that there's very little of this I do not already know. Oh, a detail or two, perhaps, which I'm sure will complete the picture. But in the main, the matter has been solved. The fact is, I have had the criminals in hand, since shortly after midnight!'

Holmes flashed me a look of apprehension. 'Oh, really?'

'Yes! I received your wire, thank you, and I do admit that it put us squarely on the track. Truth is, however, we did not have far to cast our net. Both Langdon and Sanders were arrested when they turned up at their lodgings — and have since confessed to everything.'

'Good Lord!' I said, nearly spilling my cup. 'What an unexpected turn of events!'

'Almost providential, wouldn't you say?' Holmes observed, a downcast look upon his face. 'Rather, I suspect, it is a most ingenious ploy. — But pray, Inspector, have a chair! With your permission, I shall give you our account, after which we shall hear of yours. The exchange, I'm sure, can only benefit us both.'

For the next quarter-hour, Holmes relayed to Lestrade and Mycroft what had transpired the night before: how, after divining the true intent of Moriarty's convoluted scheme, we had lain in wait for him at the National Gallery, only to be taken prisoner ourselves and transported down river to one of his haunts, where ensued the dramatic struggle that had nearly cost us our lives.

'A remarkable story, to be sure,' the policeman said, after Holmes had finished. 'Not that I doubt your word, sir. But it does contradict, in many ways, the statement which I was given.'

'Ah, does it now? Tell me, then. To what, exactly, have these men admitted?'

'Why the entire business, of course!' Lestrade declared. 'They, and the accomplice Potter — who I've no doubt, we shall soon apprehend — were behind the Crimson Vandals' game. The motive was profit, quick and substantial. Contrary to your suspicions, the art dealer Jacobsen was no innocent. In fact, he was a confederate — who had secured a means of passage for the stolen *objets d'art* on to the Continent.'

Holmes turned away to hide his disgust, and reached for his cherrywood pipe atop the mantel, which I knew gave clue as to his mood. 'But, of course,' he murmured, as he began to fill the bowl. 'How foolish of me not to see it.'

Lestrade seemed clearly pleased. 'Ah, well,' he said, 'I would not feel too badly. We cannot all be right on every count, I do suppose! — At any rate, from what they've told us, the haul was to have been far larger than a single painting. However, when you and Dr Watson surprised them, they decided to take the Greuze and flee. Assuming, I expect that we were close behind.'

'Then that much, at least, you have to thank us for,' Holmes remarked, as he struck a match and inhaled deeply, sending a blue cloud of smoke about his head.

Lestrade carefully applied a spoonful of jam to his toast, letting the silence hang. 'I will only say, consider it fortunate you both escaped,' he said. 'You say they took you to Limehouse; their story is that they dropped you in the street, unharmed, a short distance from Stepney Station. What's a jury to say? Who knows. The point is, in future, I would advise that you include Scotland Yard in your plans.'

Anger welled up inside me; this was too much! I could contain myself no longer. 'Why, this is preposterous!' I exploded. 'How dare you take the word of those criminals as equal to our own! Their story is nothing more than a flimsy fabrication! What of the attempt on the life of Sherlock Holmes? And Jacobsen's death? — Not to mention the murder of Ulric, the acrobat!'

'Here now, Doctor!' Lestrade shot back. 'Calm yourself! I'm not saying what Mr Holmes told me didn't happen. But put yourself in my position: I must have proof. Your friend has many enemies, as we all know. And, outside his theories, I've no evidence that Ulric's death is connected to any of this.'

'And Jacobsen?' I pressed.

'At this point, I suspect there was some sort of falling out among them. It's common in these sort of cases. My birds, of course, deny all knowledge of this killing. But, I imagine, it will come out in time. Perhaps once the artist Potter has also been put in gaol.'

'Well, then,' Holmes said, 'all else

withstanding, you seem to be on top of things. I have but one question for you, Inspector: what of Moriarty?'

Lestrade frowned, and put down his cup. 'I am aware of your predisposition towards that fellow,' he replied. 'As to my prisoners — they deny all knowledge of the man. Frankly, at this point, I have nothing in my grasp save your suspicions. It's hardly enough to warrant an arrest, much less hope for a conviction.'

'Ah, you have spoken to him then?' Holmes asked. 'If so, it would certainly disclaim our tale.' I knew what he was seeking.

'No,' Lestrade admitted, 'I have not. I was at his door not an hour ago, but his housekeeper said he was gone. He has been in Croydon the last three days on business, she said, but was expected to return tomorrow. You may be sure that when he does I shall question him extensively.'

Fresh clouds swirled forth from my friend's slender cherrywood. He was, I knew, as deeply frustrated and disheartened by all of this as I. Barring something unforeseen, Moriarty had slipped the net again. That is, if he were still alive. Langdon, clearly, had survived his icy plunge into the Thames. But what of the professor?

'Then at this point, I think there is little more that can be said,' Holmes concluded, turning his attentions to our crackling fire. 'My congratulations, Inspector! You have, it seems, added yet another feather to your cap — as for me, I do have some morning calls to make. You will appraise me of fresh developments?'

The policeman moved quickly to fetch his coat and hat, looking very ill at ease. The cold dismissal in Holmes's final words had been impossible for him to miss. 'I shall,' he answered, officiously, as he prepared himself for the cold. 'Understand me, Mr Holmes. I am not discounting your story, but it does not have a leg to stand on. I, on the other hand, have both crime and motive — attested to by signed confessions! Well, I must be off. Good day.'

'He's right, you know,' Mycroft said, once Lestrade had gone. I had almost forgotten he was present, since all this time he sat quietly by, content with his toast and coffee.

'Come now!' Holmes retorted, sharply. 'You surely don't believe that silly story?'

'Not a word, Sherlock. Not a word. But I do understand the inspector's dilemma. True, he could arrest Moriarty. But to what gain — save his eventual embarrassment? As it is, he at least has two of the criminals in tow, the Home Secretary is wildly happy, and the French have back their painting.'

'Ah! All's right with the world, you mean?'

'To some extent, yes.' Mycroft threw up his corpulent hands. 'You gambled and lost, Sherlock!' he exclaimed. 'That's the nub of it! Had you nabbed the fellow at the gallery, well, that's another story.'

A look of weary resignation crossed Holmes's face. 'You are right, of course,' he admitted. 'But I do not regret my course of action. It was our only chance.'

'Quite so, quite so.' With some difficulty, Mycroft shoved his massive frame up from the chair, a look of concern in his watery, grey eyes. 'You realise Moriarty is still alive?'

'Of course. Why else their move to screen him?'

'He is a much more subtle and resourceful foe than most criminals of the street,' Mycroft said. 'You must be on constant guard, Sherlock. I worry for your safety.'

'I doubt if the professor will try anything soon,' Holmes remarked. 'He is like a man who has tried to snatch something from the fire. By raising the stakes, he nearly lost his life. No, unless I have him in a corner, I doubt if he'll be so bold again.'

Mycroft reached for his coat and hat. 'Then take my advice,' he offered. 'Draw back for now. Take months, years if need be, to learn all you can about every facet of his organisation. That way, when he does finally make that tiniest of slips, you will be in a position to close the net. If you wish to work through me, I am at your service. I can supply agents, and the means.'

'With, or without the Home Secretary's knowledge?' I asked.

'I should imagine, with,' Mycroft answered. 'I am to meet with His

Lordship at two o'clock this afternoon, to report on the Crimson Vandals' affair, and to deliver him the painting, so he may in turn hand it to the French ambassador. I am quite certain, in the course of our conversation, that I shall make him aware of this latest plague upon our community.'

'Thank God,' I murmured. 'Perhaps, now, something will be done.'

After shaking hands, we escorted Holmes's brother to our door, where he took the Greuze, which we had wrapped in plain brown paper to protect it from the weather. 'Take heart, gentlemen!' he encouraged us. 'What was it Hesiod wrote? How 'Often an entire city has suffered because of an evil man.' Hopefully, through Sherlock's wit, and the sword of British justice, we shall not suffer long.'

I could not help but wonder, as the portly minister without portfolio descended our oft-trod stairs, where this struggle between good and evil would end. There was no way of knowing that what Mycroft had proposed, would indeed eventually come to pass. That, working with government agents, Holmes would one day finally be able to weave a net from which even the wily professor could not escape, bringing about more assassination attempts and their final duel at Reichenbach.[1] That time, thankfully, no one would be there to pull him from the abyss.

★   ★   ★

'Merry Christmas, Holmes!' I said, as we raised our glasses of Montrachet.

My final words on the Crimson Vandals' affair must be dated Christmas Eve, 1888. Outside, soft flakes of snow were gently floating down amidst the street lights, and we could faintly hear the sound of carollers somewhere below. Mrs Hudson had outdone herself — presenting us with a holiday meal of succulent goose, and buttered carrots laced with gravy, accompanied by custard tarts and apple cake.

Our plan that night was not to venture

---

[1] *The Final Problem*, April 24-May 4, 1891.

far from our crackling fire. Holmes wore his purple dressing gown, I my usual maroon with black lapels. Cigars and brandy, and our exchange of gifts, were still ahead.

No wonder then, I was surprised when my friend put down his glass, and from beneath the table produced a brightly-wrapped package, which he thrust into my hands.

'Surely, Holmes,' I said, 'this can wait until later.'

'No, Watson,' he assured me. 'It is something we shall toast again, after you have seen.'

Tearing open the paper, I found before me, elegantly framed and matted, that passage from the Greek Apocrypha:

A faithful friend is a strong defence; and he that has found such an one hath found a treasure.

Ecclesiasticus, 6:14

It has hung upon my bedroom wall to this day.